"*Do you play that?*"

A man's voice asked from the shadows.

Stunned, I took a step back and my annoying cloak marked the movement with a flurry of chimes. He leaned against a pillar in the shadows, dressed from head to toe like a genuine, roughened cowboy. An unlit cigarette was clamped between his full lips, he tipped his head indicating the flute.

"Um, n-no, I don't play. I'm not a musician," I rambled.

The dark leather hat was tipped back in old-world courtesy, allowing me to glimpse more of his beautiful black face. On his squared jaw, a light bristle caught the light, but I could see his eyes were keen on me like a lion on distant prey.

Well, I'll be damned if it wasn't my nemesis, Brad, from the licensing department! His smile turned into a lecherous grin that carried entirely too much sex appeal. The flutter that had started in my gut tightened.

At work, I argued with this man at least twice a day, often condemning his entire gene pool and cursing his questionable ancestry. But since day one, the attraction between us had been undeniable, sparking like a match in a room full of gunpowder.

Indigo Love Stories

presented by Genesis Press Publishing

Genesis Press, Inc.
315 Third Avenue North
Columbus, MS 39701

Reviews for Ebony Butterfly 1

5 out of 5 Rawsistaz Review

Powerful, intoxicating erotica

Author Delilah Dawson provides us with powerful, intoxicating erotica in Ebony Butterfly II. Her latest collection of short stories, it is an offering of erotica at many different levels with stories that will definitely please readers of all backgrounds.

The stories in Ebony Butterfly II are fresh and captivating. From beginning to end we are introduced to a variety of different characters in interesting but sexy scenarios. From several executives at a "Masquerade" to a young store clerk "Bent For Leather", each story carries a passionate, sensual twist that will keep readers alike turning the pages. Even a romantic tip or two can be picked up from these stories.

Overall Ms. Dawson does an amazing job with Ebony Butterfly II, providing readers with stories that are both hot and unique. Both men and women will enjoy this collection, and it is one that is great to read with a lover nearby. Ms. Dawson definitely ranks among the levels with author Zane, and she is truly one to watch. I look forward to more works from Ms. Dawson.

4 out of 4 Romantic Times Magazine

Extremely erotic in it's content, EBONY BUTTERFLY is by far the best-written work in the Indigo After Dark series thus far. With refreshing characters, tense sensuality, perfect chemistry and creative foreplay, Dawson definitely delivers a sexy tale. (Sep, 161 pp, $14.95)

Dedication

"To my husband, for everything, with much love."

"visit my web site at www.delilahdawson.com"
-Delilah Dawson

Ebony Butterfly Volume II

by
Delilah Dawson

Genesis Press, Inc.

DELILAH DAWSON

Solstice Offering

In the rural meadow that is my backyard, I lay in the temple of Solstice Goddess awaiting the ceremony. Overhead, a frail lilac moon gleams, watering softly over the landscape with its paleness.

Grass Valley is beautiful this time of year. There are fields upon fields surrounding my house, and on March nights like this, at the cusp of spring, the grass looks like flowing velvet, the wind is gentle, and the landscape becomes almost mystical.

The small temple I lay in was built with the stark, elegant simplicity of functional architecture and a few pieces of primitive African art. The snake-shaped mahogany pillars holding up the roof represent the Dinka goddess, Abuk. A small statue of Ala, Nigerian earth mother and goddess of fertility, sits at one corner. Domfe, god of rain and wind, perches from the rafters. And in the center is the largest piece. A Nubian idol created in the bountiful image of the great African goddess Yemoja.

All of them wait.

Only sliding rice-paper doors shield the entities from the rest of the world.

The Initiator created everything, from the goddess to the ceremony. Part of the ceremony, he'd said, was from traditions handed down from his farming ancestors. The rest he had made up, guided by some inexplicable spiritual need.

I have come to develop a great respect for that.

I had been doing research on African rituals when I met him a year ago. Fascinated by his doctorate and his intensity, I had been so curious, wanting to know... What I'd found was an intellectual with primal tendencies.

I smiled to myself. Ahhh, that was seasons ago...

Now, I lay at the foot of the large, robust goddess, envying her abundant breasts, her sunflower-sized nipples, her enormous fertile girth. Her face revealed a study of ecstasy, eyes half-open, lips parted, cheeks taut as if crying out.

Earlier, I dutifully placed chosen fruits and vegetables in her hands above her head and lit the candles by her spread knees. Between them, her open thighs revealed her deep, open vagina, beautiful and luscious as a rare bearded orchid.

The coolness of the wood seeped into my naked back, causing a shiver to run through me. It raised goose bumps on my flesh, tightened my nipples and birthed a brook within my sex that moistened a path from my womb to the base of my fresh flower.

Where is he? Why is he making me wait? I could feel the deities watching me, expectantly, their gazes familiar.

Caving in to my impatience, I touched my vagina, finding the wet folds, caressing my heated bud, rubbing inside the slickness and inhaling the seafoam fragrance of its bloom.

A ripple of breeze murmured over grass and whispered into my ear like the breath of a lover. With my eyes slipping shut, I opened my legs wider, plucking at the dwarfed stamen of my clitoris, plunging my eager fingers between my thickening petals for more. Shifting my buttocks against the wood, I rubbed harder, wanting to feel the thunder that was building a flood within me.

With a start, the single creak of wood alerted me to his presence, jolting my system with adrenaline. I immediately stopped my exploration, but was yet unable to stop panting.

He stepped out of the shadows, dark as the moonlight would allow, completely naked. His limbs glistened with a thin sheen of perspiration, and I could easily make out his clean-shaven head as he watched me.

He stood, like a carnal panther, like forces of ten thousand shadows incarnate. The contouring muscles of his body pitted the light in places, weaving shadows of strength and making flowing patterns of his valleys and plains.

Gold bands strapped around his brawny arms reminded me of tribal warriors. Matte black pubic hair glistened, accentuating the wider, stronger stance of his legs and his torso. His elongated penis reached for me, like a beggar for a handout.

"You should have waited," he rebuked huskily.

"I-I-I could not," I said as I hurried to kneel upright beside the statue, in the position I should have been in all along.

He turned away from me and reached behind the head of the goddess, hitting a hidden knob. Immediately, a soft hum was heard and a quiet shower of water poured from the numerous sprinklers that covered the ceiling, alternating between hot, warm and cold drops.

Domfe, god of rain, breathed.

Only the tiny umbrellas in the candles kept the gentle flames from flickering out.

As the water sluiced over him, I watched him start the ceremony. He kissed the parted mouth of the goddess with quiet reverence, then moved his hands over her water-bathed breasts, touching the unmoving bronze as if they were real, then at the crux of her thighs, he inserted his penis into the cavity, filling the mouth of her flower to the hilt.

I watched the drizzle of water playing with the illusion of shadow and form until both he and the statue seemed as one, locked in a moment of lustful passion. My innards tightened sharply, as if he was possessing me instead of the inanimate object.

He groaned, and I could see the tight muscular grip of his buttocks as he clenched, shoved once, then stepped away. Like light over a blade, a glimmer revealed the cock ring that now banded the base of his beautiful phallus.

He reached past the offerings to the crown of the goddess where he extracted a long phallic gourd, bronzed and shiny with ritual use. When he turned to me, I immediately went to the center of the room and leaned forward, on all fours. He came to stand before me until my face was by his feet. With one hand, he leaned on the base of my spine and with the other, he introduced the rigid form into my exposed vagina, pushing hard into my tight passage, where nothing had been in more than three months.

I moaned at the intense pleasure, feeling the cold rain like shower on my spine, the cold wood against my breasts. Still he pushed, the invasion turning hotter as it was crammed deep within me.

Satisfied with the depth of penetration, he ordered me to kneel and sit back, which I did. The fat remainder of the gourd nestled like a seat between my ankles.

He then walked behind me, squatting slowly against me, the plum ripe roughness of his penis trailing down my spine, slippery with water. His hands sank into my hair and there was the slightest tug before he moved his cock upward again. Slowly...slowly...

I could only imagine the strain on his thigh muscles at the controlling movements.

Once he reached the top, his hands clenched my hair, circled my neck, then with a soft touch, he trailed his palms over my collarbone, over to my shoulders, his callused fingertips leaving a delightful friction. I shivered, feeling the exquisite mixture of his hot touch and the sluicing coolness of the pseudo rain.

Against my back, the suede-softness of his testicles now trailed more urgently at the wake of his penis.

Against my front his hands moved toward my breasts as he began his descent of my spine again.

I rocked against the gourd lodged between my legs. By now it was covered with the fluids of my eagerness and the lubrication wedged it further, wider into me. He kept moving up and down my spine, pulling my hands over my head so that they could go around his neck. His wide palms caressed my armpits, breasts, ribs, navel, trailing the water as it fell over me. Down, down until he could fondle my stuffed sex.

I moaned, the sound coming out pained. His inquisitive fingers began to rub my clitoris in a circular, three-fingered movement.

I clutched at his shaved head, shamelessly jutting my hips against his thick fingers and rocking harder against the phallic gourd, bumping backward against his erection. He teased his fingers around the stalk of the gourd, stretching my labia around it, rocking me with soft pushes that mated me to it until I could hardly think.

With the strength of a phantom sneeze, I climaxed on a quivering cry, still moving frantically against the delicious friction inside and outside me. At that moment, I could've been the goddess herself, incoherent with ecstasy. Light-headed, my head fell back against him and it was several seconds before I could feel rain on my face and open mouth.

Together we rocked as one, him holding me close in an embrace that both supported me and impaled me farther onto the gourd. So close were we that I could feel nothing at my back but his flesh and the throb of his trapped sex like a tubular root at the curve of my buttocks.

His fight for control quaked against me, but he didn't penetrate me, nor did he ejaculate.

Over and over the spray of water washed over us, hot, cold then as tepid as the dew of tropical cascades.

Shifting me onto his lap, he removed the gourd with a twist and set it aside. I was so limp, I could do nothing more than whimper as one strong arm banded around me to clasp one breast while the other hand plunged into me, harvesting my juices. His breathing deepened further when he began sucking the silky handful as if it was a decadent nectar. Each dip served to feed him, in a hum of consent.

Then me.

With my wetness on his fingertips, he anointed a path upon my breasts, my navel, my waist, down to my inner thighs... And still my river flowed with each sensitive aftermath.

When his breathing snagged and his hold became painful, I suddenly understood how close he was to cumming, and it gave me the strength to kneel again. His harsh breath brushed my ear as his lips briefly found my neck, nipping and kissing me there in thanks.

The soft, chimelike song of water filled the silence while he walked around to stand before me. I could hear the heavier splattering sounds as the water slipped over our elevated temple to the ground below.

I found myself swallowing eagerly at the sight of his erection. I sucked in a breath, tasting airborne pheromones and smelling the musky maleness of his sex. I parted my mouth and let the taste of his rain-drenched foreskin reach my lips.

Following the presentation of my tongue, he held my head in both his hands and penetrated my mouth the way he had initiated the goddess.

I cupped his buttocks and took his meaty length so deep that I had to fight a reflex gag. Even then, his hands tightened on my scalp and he shoved into me almost involuntarily, causing my teeth to scrape against the silver cock-ring. I forced my throat to relax, to take it.

In... Then out... In, then out. In then out. In. Out. In. In. In...

His movement went from slow pauses to faster, less controlled thrusts. His testicles slapped wetly against my chin and my tightened nipples grazed his thighs. His breathing became grunts when I reached to stroke his twin testicles, slippery now from saliva and drizzling water.

I worked my tongue around him, sucked my cheeks to further caress him, opened my throat to accommodate him until my jaw was practically numb. Moments stretched where nothing existed but the sorcery of his foreign, unintelligible rough murmurs, the audience of gods and the unequivocal seduction of submitting to these throatiest of kisses.

I started to taste the loamy drops of his ejaculation and hurried to unclench the cock ring. It had barely clicked apart when he surged into me like a wild beast, his coarse cry matching the moment that his semen shot into the recess of my mouth.

I swallowed against his pulsating length, fighting for breath against his rigid hold on my head.

He stood before me barely thrusting, even though his legs trembled. Minutes passed where he gulped for air, his penis deflating in my mouth.

Finally, he let it slip out and we lay together under the soft waterfall.

Lazily we kissed each other, tasting our sexes on our breath, and feeling the distant sparks of arousal. Hands were permitted to roam, to caress, to clutch anywhere.

When I felt the unmistakable re-awakening of his penis against my thigh, he reversed our position, so I could tongue his soft-hard length while he sought to taste the waters of my brook.

My stretched pool was so sensitive, I could hardly focus on his member when his fingers and tongue worked into me. An especially hard thrust of fingers caused me to unintentionally clench my teeth against his now-rigid length.

He immediately changed our positions, pinning my hands over my head. I'd waited three whole months, longing for this very moment and when he thrust forcefully between my parted thighs, my world shimmered brightly in silver, threatening to fall apart.

I arched my back, trying to take a length that was bigger and wider than the ceremonial gourd. For that one primal moment, I was woman, my soul discovering a place and time where our joining created a perfect universe.

He dominated me with an uncompromising tempo until I felt I would not exist if not for his shaft cleaving me and his weight upon me. I could barely see through the smattering of water drops, and with every surge and thrust, water trailed over his shoulders, falling like tears over me.

"Please," I begged, writhing as I worked to crest the peak of the emotional storm that raged inside me.

I couldn't breathe when he kissed me again, but by then I didn't care about anything but the savage, wet meter of our joining, until silver turned to gold behind my eyes.

The first touch of the goddess hit me like a wave, clutching him in my trembling womb. He jammed his weight against me as I bucked weakly, stammering for him to never stop.

Trapped as I was, his thrusts had now become closely timed punts and nudges. Time passed in minutes or even hours, before he finally flipped me over, bringing me on all fours and taking me the way an impatient and arrogant stallion ravages a flirtatious mare. Even the slippery wetness of my body didn't dislocate the strong grip of his hands on my hips.

Only for him did I keep my knees together, round my ass and submit to the pelvic plundering, feeling the pleasure-pain mingle strongly with the sensitive rawness of my passage. My breasts jostled and I almost fell on my face when the final rippling heat of his ejaculation caused my womb to spasm unexpectedly.

With my muscles too fatigued to stay upright, I slipped down to my belly, carrying him on my back, our bodies still languidly joined. We lay like prone sex slaves before the solstice goddess, listening to our breaths and heartbeats amid the drizzle of rain.

When the cold wind turned the warm drops into uncomfortable tears, he withdrew from me, kissing me with detached veneration. Every part of me was touched with his lips, from my mouth, my breasts, my spine, my vagina, all the way to the soles of my feet.

"The goddess should be pleased," he whispered when he covered me again, his voice gentle and beholden. "We should have a good crop this season."

I held him close, unwilling to admit that the ceremony was now officially over.

Bent for Leather

Having allergies has got to be one of the worst experiences ever, don't you think? Well, if you've ever had them, honey, you'd agree. I was constantly walking around with watery eyes, runny nose and sneezing, looking like a fool.

But, finally, my doctor gave me a new prescription I had to squirt in my nose. Nasal bath, he called it, giving me one of those smiles that made his nose hairs stick out. The sight reminded me to ask him about side effects, to which he said, "Oh, they're minimal, hardly noticeable." Sure, this from a man who obviously never smiled at himself in the mirror!

Anyway, I was desperate enough to try the spray, and I'm glad to say that my allergies have indeed gone, and thank heavens, my nose still looks normal. But about a month ago, I began to realize some of the side effects were sexual! I found almost carnal joy in inhaling, breathing in scents that not only evoked memories but aroused sensations.

For example, the smell of leather.

Okay, I work at a men's shoe store, so this was probably the reason for that, but I'm embarrassed to say that I really enjoy it. I'd find myself shelving the new shoes and suddenly the smell of leather would remind me of the taste of sweat during sex, or of pubic hair or all sorts of other passionate tastes. It got to the point that I had to find some privacy before I opened a box, allowing the intimate smell of foot apparel to quietly assault me, seduce me.

Shameless, I know!

I even found myself at a western apparel and tack store one day, like a pervert on the prowl. Time and again, my eyes drifted to the black, intricately designed saddle by the door, wondering how the leather would feel between the spread of my legs, against the softness of my thighs. What would the dry, abrasive touch of suede feel like against my skin? Would it feel different if it was wet? Would it smell differently?

So on my last doctor's visit, I happily told him there were no side effects, no sir, none! I grabbed the prescription and headed out the door before I could remember I owed money for my co-payment.

Of course, at work, I try to remain professional. I insist on helping all my customers, courteously sitting them down, studying and measuring their feet and then showcasing their various shoe selections by putting them on their feet.

Since my store caters mostly to executives, their feet are usually clad in silk or nylon socks. And let me tell you, the stench of stinky feet could haunt me for hours!

It was a slow day when Mr. Jones, one of my repeat customers, walked into my store. He usually visits right after our new shipment of shoes comes in.

Normally, I wear a formal business suit because my nipples always perk up prominently whenever I'm aroused, which means most of the time. But since it had been a slow day and almost closing time, I had removed my business jacket...a move I regretted the moment I saw Mr. Jones.

For a long time now, I had a suspicion that he knew about my turn-ons, but he remained unfailingly polite. He was the consummate executive but had the build of a runner. He looked clean-cut and middle-aged, speaking with a quiet, slight southern accent. Ever the professional, I offered him a seat and a beverage, which was always iced water. His instructions, given in a deep rum-and-coffee voice, were always no-nonsense, but personable.

"I'll try those in black, then the Versace in navy blue."

I hurried to comply. My assistant had left early for the day, so I was left to single-handedly cater to this man. I retrieved the boxes, then knelt at his feet to remove his shoes. From my vantage point, I could smell him; his clothes, his cologne, the talcum powder he used on his feet. But more than that, I smelled something that was unique to him...something that drew me every time, intoxicating.

I sat at his feet, trying not to touch his flawless olive-green pants. On the armrest, his pristine white shirt was rolled up at the sleeves, revealing strong forearms. I could smell the unique scent of his body heat from the blistering day outside.

Reaching for a shoe horn beneath his chair, I leaned closer, imagining his more intimate smells...his pubic smell...something like suede.

I licked my lips and played with the fantasy of burying my face in his lap to inhale his scent. It was a light mustiness that smelled as if he'd recently washed his penis, then decided to masturbate.

An excellent, arousing scent.

And as my mama would say, I'm going straight to hell for thinking that way. Except I wasn't thinking of mama or hell or anything but the possibility of where my mind was taking me.

It made my mouth water.

My fingers fumbled on his shoe, and I looked up to see his intent gaze on my bountiful cleavage, then up to my eyes, a knowing smile on his face.

"What do you think of it?" he asked.

I studied the shoe but peripherally I noticed an erection forming in his business pants. "They're beautiful shoes."

"Yes...and just the right fit."

My nipples could not have been more puckered had I been in the middle of the Antarctic. My breathing had altered to something a bit embarrassing, and I had a feeling my face was showing an aroused blush as well.

"Put the other one on," he instructed, so I went about doing so. Jeez, I was starting to lose it, wondering if his beautiful feet would be bold enough to creep up my leg from beneath a dinner table and rub it provocatively against my clitoris.

"Thank you," he said when I'd finished. Then he stood as if to test the shoes out. But he didn't move, and from my position, his now blatant erection was inches from my face.

"Hmm," he said huskily as he put his hands on his hips. "I'd like to see the Garvanchi in gray. Do you have them?"

For a second, all I could do was stare stupidly at his zipper. I was breathing softly through my mouth and I could've sworn I tasted his sexual pheromones upon my lips. "Garvanchi, right! Ah, I can check the back room."

"Yes, let's..."

I heard the subtle auto lock on the front door, triggered by the closing mechanism, telling me it was six-thirty on the dot. My business day was officially over.

For those few seconds, reason cleared my head and I was tempted to tell Mr. Jones to show up the next day. When it started to become apparent that I was wavering, I smiled politely and nervously lead Mr. Jones to the back room, into my world of olfactory delights, leather and absolutely no pair of Garvanchis in gray. I knew that for a fact, but couldn't stop myself from leading him that way.

Having committed to this point, I pretended to search for them for a few minutes, then returned to where he stood, offering him a pair in black. "There's none in gray, sir."

"I'd like to try these on. Please put them on me," he muttered, almost a lazy whisper.

Again I knelt before him, smelling him again, sensing where things were heading and unable to stop the mixture of dread and arousal that flowed thickly in my veins. Removing the earlier shoes, I went about putting on the new ones. The still room echoed the soft shuffling sounds, expanding the tension until I had to briefly close my eyes. I was almost finished when I felt his hand in my hair, the touch soft and coaxing.

"There's some discomfort," he murmured.

I looked up slowly, letting my eyes travel over the formal crease of his pants, up to his seriously large erection that was now less than an inch from my lips, on upward to where his eyes were daring me. I swallowed dryly, audibly, know-ing that I wanted to give him the pleasure he sought, knowing I wanted to taste the flavors I smelled. His eyes narrowed marginally and again I saw that scorching challenge in his heated gaze.

Two soul-searching seconds later, I made up my mind.

"Allow me," I whispered and reached for his belt. The delicate clink of the buckle filled the silence, the unleashed hush of the belt as I loosened it through the first loop made me shiver with need. Giving in to my growing urges, I cupped his bulge over the material, massaging his balls and firm length. Every single pulse point in me wanted him, wanted to be exactly where I was, antic-ipating the outcome.

Mr. Jones groaned in one long breath. His hand on my hair tightened as I moved my fingers over the zipper, tugging it downward. The not-so-quiet metallic teeth of his zipper unraveled his package like a sensual gift. His scent and size rose up to meet me, and I found myself awed, admiring his restrained phallus and the musky smell as I licked my lips, preparing to taste. The broth-er was definitely packaged!

Without a word I pulled both his white Calvin Klein underwear and his pants downward until they sagged around his ankles. His grip on my hair tugged me forward, and I gave in to my deepest fantasies, burying my face in his crotch and inhaling deeply. Sighing shakily, I let my lips tentatively touch the hot, long, rigid flesh of his cock, licking a moist, tasty path toward the turgid head of his penis where the plum-sized head was flushed as tight as an eggplant, expecting to be sucked.

As I licked the underside of his penis, a blue vein pulsed against my tongue, its throb causing the penis to strain further. I rubbed my palm against his bul-bous testicles, weighing them, caressing them. All the smells turned into liq-uid fire in my veins.

Mr. Jones had thrown his head back to lean against the wall, and I could hear him breathing hard. His cock was mine now, I thought lustily, all mine! I felt absolutely starved for it, so I teased the hard length, licking long, lavish licks, tasting the flavors that, until this moment, I had only dreamed of. My teeth gently nipped him and he momentarily jolted, but I made it up to him by licking his testicles and using my lips to suck them partially into my mouth. Mr. Jones ground out a profanity between his groans and a tremble snaked over his body. Once his testicles were suitably wet, I began to tease his cock again without actually sucking it. I was rewarded with a pre-cum drop that I licked right up.

"Suck," he ordered, sounding pained and aroused. "Now! Suck!"

I obeyed, parting my lips and allowing him to surge into my mouth in a carnal thrust. Mr. Jones' hand worked against my scalp, tugging me into a rhythm that lubricated his formidable rise as quickly as the juices dripping between my thighs. Greedily, I moaned, or rather, I hummed while my tongue swirled around him, taking his snake length as it pushed toward my tonsils. Each thrust meant a tighter grip in my hair and a deeper insertion down my throat. His sex smell was just as delicious as I had imagined, while the rest of him seemed to become too big for comfortable fellatio.

"Yes," he groaned in approval. His thrusts were uncompromising, face-fucking me until I could barely work my lips and mouth around his unstoppable tempo. "Yes...suck it!...yes...deeper...harder...yes... stroke my balls...yes...ah, God...yes..."

I could feel the tremor in his thighs as he got closer to his orgasm. Kneeling as I was, I squeezed my thighs together, heightening my own pleasure where my clitoris throbbed.

By now his cock was pumping into my mouth like a slippery piston, assaulting my need to breathe, thickening ever so slightly between my lips as his cum gathered and curled in his balls.

Already I could taste the first drops like seawater and lemonade in my mouth. My left hand joined the stroke of my mouth, mimicking the drag and suck of my lips. My right hand stroked his saliva-moistened balls in tandem to his grunting thrusts. My cheeks and jaw ached as I braced myself for the impending moment.

Two gagging thrusts later, he grunted like a mounted bull and his cum spilled hot and wicked into the back of my throat. I thought I'd been prepared but it filled my mouth in such a large dose that some of it slipped past my lips. I breathed hard through my nostrils, working my mouth eagerly, desperate that I would miss a single runaway drop. In my hand, his testicles shriveled for a split second as the final spurts squirted weakly onto my tongue.

I was thrilled that I had got him off in my mouth, but now my body was tense, demanding its own relief, but because of his grip in my hair, I was forced to stay in my subservient position while his rocking came to a halt. With his masterful penis in my mouth, I leisurely swirled my tongue, feeling it shrivel back to its normal size.

Finally, he removed his hand and I let his sex slip out from between my lips.

"You've been most accommodating," he said huskily.

I couldn't believe how uninhibited and liberated I felt. "I aim to please," I replied sassily, still swallowing some of the taste of him lingering in my mouth. A thin sheen of sweat covered his face, and he was still breathing heavily.

"Now, be a good girl and go brace yourself against that table."

My body was craving sex so badly, I hurried to do as he said, placing my hands on the worktable, pushing my hips out and waiting. I heard his clothes rustle as he approached from behind.

Around me the air was an aphrodisiac mixture of sex, flesh and leather. The different swatch samples of leather colors lay by my hand, tools of the trade were scattered around on the surface of the table. I focused on the bottles of refined oils I'd used to polish the display shoes. Without explanation, I felt taunted by them. My body felt on fire, turning into a fluid heat that burned from the depths of my womb to my swollen vaginal lips.

Mr. Jones came up behind me and pushed my short lilac skirt over my hips, revealing my garters and lilac-colored French lacy undies. I held my breath as several seconds passed.

I felt his eyes at the very center of my exposed sex as I waited, nervous and primed to anticipation. His reserved, executive shoes tapped my inner heels, indicating I should spread my legs wider.

So I did.

And still he tormented me with waiting. When I least expected it, his fingers dug under the scrap of cloth covering my crotch, his hard knuckles rubbing against me as he wrestled his fingers into my wet center, in a full-knuckled thrust. I must have cried out at the intense pleasure, but I was deaf and blind to everything but that widening entry.

"Shhh..." With a sudden jerk, his fingers curled around my undies and he ripped them off. Now that the obstacle was removed, his hand resumed the fornicating act, moved in and out at a longer, harder pace. I whimpered like a weak puppy and resorted to biting my lip but I couldn't hold back my moans. God, his fingers felt so good!

"You want more, don't you?" He removed his hand to reach for one of the tools on the bench. The shoe stretcher. It had a long ribbed cherrywood grip that suddenly looked like a beautifully crafted dildo. Why had I never noticed that before?

He then reached for an unopened pack of chamois. Not just any pack. This was the special-order moose-suede rags I'd ordered from Canada. Each sterile rag was tan and as thin and soft as silk. And they cost a freaking fortune.

Both items were moved out of my line of vision, but my imagination went into overdrive at the sounds Mr. Jones was making with them.

When he finally touched me, it was with a hard foreign presence that brushed against the lips of my slippery vagina. With each pass of the rigid object, I came to realize he'd secured the suede over the ribbed handle and was now lubricating it on my juices. He twirled it over my labia then pushed it against my swollen lips teasingly, brushing the length of it up, then down and around, infuriating me when he avoided penetration. Again he did this. And again...and again...

By now the suede felt sufficiently saturated and its leathery texture became a tonguelike caress that made me rock against the delightfully unexpected licks. With an expert touch, Mr. Jones began to whirl it in half insertions, half-feeding my sex-starved cunt.

"Ahh, God!" I pleaded.

The half inch became two, then three, whirling and twisting in and out until I was withstanding ten long, solid fucking inches of suede and leather from the shoe-spreader's handle. My greedy sex suckled on the pseudo-cock like my mouth had done on Mr. Jones' shaft.

"Oh, please," I begged as I rocked faster against the rhythm of his hand.

"Slow down..." he murmured as he bent over me. "Slow down..."

I tried to, I really did, but I was enjoying how he was plowing it into me, working the suede dildo at an aggravating slow, rough pace, so deep it throbbed like a colossal tongue inside me, and when he withdrew it, it tugged at me from the inside until I could've sobbed.

His free hand began to torment my clitoris with round turns that sent shivers up my spine. Ruthlessly he kept the slower pace, knocking against my G-spot as I wiggled and whimpered, trying to enter the orgasm zone.

The sopping, sloppy-wet sounds of his shoves became noisier. In and out it went, jabbing deeper and yanking out harder, making me feel raw and depraved as I begged and begged.

I felt myself coming closer to my release as the tremors rushed like electricity against my breasts, my clit, my parted lips. "M-M-Misssster Jones!"

I could hardly think, speak or breathe after that, because he removed the dildo and replaced it with his swollen rigid shaft, picking up the pace and ramming into me, faster and faster, launching me headfirst into a deep abdominal spasm that made me buck and grit my teeth as my body pulsed out a wave of orgasmic sensation.

The burst of it held me in its grip for several seconds and even then, the pounding continued, becoming softer, until I fell against the table, too weak and quivering to do anything else.

I looked over my shoulder and saw Mr. Jones with his head thrown back in a stark mask of ecstasy as his magnificent erection erupted deep inside me. I thought he might fall, but amazingly, he managed to stay upright.

Our heavy breathing echoed in the room, slowing as we recovered from passion. Moments, later, without a word, he slipped his softening penis out of me then meticulously pulled my skirt back down. With nothing better to do, I straightened and picked imaginary lint from my shirt, then ran a hand absently over my hair. By the time I was done, I could hear his belt clink as he fastened it around his waist.

When our eyes met again, he was back to being the wealthy executive client who had walked into my store for a pair of quality shoes.

I made a grasp for normalcy. "So, do you want me to order the Garvanchi shoes in gray, sir?"

He contemplated while staring at my still-perky nipples. His smile taunted, reminding me that if he said yes, he would visit my store again and I could find myself braced against the worktable, begging for another hard fuck from a shoe appliance and a leather rag. Or maybe I could get some condoms and bring some of my toys and...

"Sure," he replied. "I'll return next week and try them on to see if they're suitable."

I felt both pleasantly ashamed and yet doubly aroused. I struggled for something appropriate to say, but I felt too overwhelmed by what had just happened. I wanted to keep this mood, this mystery of our secret game. "I can arrange that," I blurted as I made the first awkward move toward the door.

Oh, yeah, straight to hell, as mama would say.

He followed me out to where he'd left his briefcase, with the smug look of a man who'd had his clever suspicions confirmed. Murmuring something about how fast time flies, I unlocked the front door and let him out. Just as I was about to lock the door behind him, his arm reached out to hold my neck, then his mouth slanted over mine in a long, lingering kiss.

When it was over, I remained in shocked surprise, watching him head toward the parking lot. The final backward wink he gave me warmed me for no apparent reason.

I finished closing up and walked back to my storage room wearing a huge grin.

Masquerade (Estelle's story)

The party had been thumping at the San Francisco estate since dusk had taken over the sky. All the guests, complete in their elaborate costumes, were dancing to the grooves and slowly losing their inhibitions as the night grew longer. I looked around, seeing that everyone from our office had dressed in what was a very likely image of their alter egos, and as a result, the dance floor was filled with vampires, pirates, ghosts and superheroes. When you work among computer programmers, the alter egos are far and wide.

I had taken a break from dancing and found myself a quiet corner, but my hiding place was disturbed when another couple came into my space without noticing me. I watched in fascination as a tall, rasta-braided vampire, dressed in a black tuxedo, wrapped his arm around a French barmaid and proceeded to nibble the nape of her neck until the woman moaned. Bolder still, his hands roamed over her breasts, molding them, caressing them and then pinching the nipples with the expert touch of a seasoned lover. When she whimpered, his mouth replaced his fingers, giving them freedom to roam behind the black-and-white apron to undo her buttons.

I could hardly believe I was watching the mail-room guy seducing one of our major associates. Her eyes were half-closed as if blinded from his touch. When he muttered something rough and ground his hips against hers, I began to feel the heat of wetness and yearning deep in my own loins.

The lazy jazz reached from the speakers like cigarette smoke, seductive and tugging at my senses even more. When the vampire shoved his hands under

20

her skirt, she muttered a soft obscenity and began to grind her hips into his hand with urgency.

Even that music couldn't hide the involuntary gasp from my lips, sending a ripple of sound from my coin-laced cloak, giving away my voyeuristic position.

The vampire glanced sharply in my direction withdrawing his hand. With his other hand clasping the skimpy skirt of the French maid, he deliberately grabbed her buttocks, tugging at the seductive fishnets. She murmured something faint but disapproving, and he reluctantly pulled her into the body of dancers that crowded the dimlit dance floor, slipping away with her.

"Damnit," I grumbled, not entirely sure if I was angry with myself for watching or because my stupid harem cloak had given me away.

The heck with this dumb outfit anyway. If I'd have known how cold the night would be, I'd have wanted more material than the gauze that barely covered my breasts and legs. But since the night was downright frosty, I was determined that no matter how noisy the cloak was, at least it kept me warm.

I pushed the carry-on flute aside, wondering for the hundredth time why the instrument was part of the rental. As far as I knew, I'd never seen harem dancers with flutes on TV, much less cloaks with bells and coins on them. My only pathetic excuse was that pickings were really slim at the rental shop.

"Do you play that?" a man's voice asked from the shadows. Stunned, I took a step back and my annoying cloak marked the movement with a flurry of chimes. He leaned against a pillar in the shadows, dressed from head to toe like a genuine, roughened cowboy. An unlit cigarette was clamped between his full lips, he tipped his head, indicating the flute.

"Um, n-no, I don't play. I'm not a musician," I rambled.

The dark leather hat was tipped back in old-world courtesy, allowing me to glimpse more of his beautiful black face. On his squared jaw, a light bristle caught the light, but I could see his eyes were keen on me like a lion on distant prey.

Well, I'll be damned if it wasn't my nemesis, Brad, from the licensing department! His smile turned into a lecherous grin that carried entirely too much sex appeal. The flutter that had started in my gut tightened.

At work, I argued with this man at least twice a day, often condemning his entire gene pool and cursing his questionable ancestry. But since day one, the attraction between us had been undeniable, sparking like a match in a room full of gunpowder.

Okay, the bastard sure was sexy! I had to give him that. And he was built like a warrior, with broad shoulders, tight thighs and a butt that made my palms itch to grab it. It was more than his looks, though. It was the way he knew how to say just the wrong thing...or the right one. It was the way he winked at me as if he knew what I was thinking. It was the way he made me feel naked just by looking at me. Like now.

The intensity in his gaze gave me the odd suspicion that he'd been watching me for quite some time, maybe since Dracula had French-kissed the maid, and I felt a blush heating my cheeks.

"I'm Buffalo Brad," he said as he stepped away from the pillar and reached my side. Over the din of conversation and jazz, I could barely make out the delicate clink of his spurs as they touched the marble tiles. As he got closer, I could smell the leather from his vest and hear the faint creak of his chaps. Maybe I was trying too hard not to notice how his crotch seemed accentuated by the overlaying leather. Trying to pretend everything was normal, I said, "Buffalo Brad, huh? I just knew rustling bull is your area of expertise.... You do it at work all the time."

His eyes narrowed as he studied me for a full minute. The hot flash of anger in his eyes changed as they began roaming over my skin like warm water, making me feel completely naked in a roomful of people. Mostly inebriated and groping people.

I looked away nervously, absently running my hand over the flute.

"Nice mouth organ you've got there," he countered. "Too bad you don't know how to play it."

I clenched my jaw and glared at him, then boldly dared to look down at his crotch, wanting to make a smart retort about his penis and my "mouth organ," but the words died in my mouth when I saw he was completely aroused and straining against the zipper of his jeans. The mere size of him dried my mouth, and I licked my lips without thinking. My pulse flickered wildly over my tongue, my breasts, unraveling like heavy potion in my loins.

He took a step closer, then another. And another. Until we stood only inches apart. I suddenly became aware of his harsh breathing, realizing the chemistry of sexual tension was filling my lungs with parched need.

"Estelle, come closer," he murmured, his voice a dark, bewitching rumble.

For a blinding second, I almost did, knowing full well what he intended, but the jazzy music abruptly ended and the silence that followed was billowing with too much daring.

Ooh! This was dangerous. Definitely no good for me! Trying to play it off, I turned and hurried away, giving him a pathetic excuse about having to find a bathroom to powder my nose. I felt like I'd turned my back on a wolf, and it took everything I had not to start running.

I knew then that I had to get out of there. I had to find my roommate, drag her to the car and get the hell out of Dodge! How could it be that three glasses of wine had almost made me show Buffalo Brad just how well I could play his mouth organ?

I definitely had to go!

I glimpsed Sara in her cheerleading outfit as she slipped into a room down the hall with a black Terminator look-alike. By the time I got there, I could hear them grappling against the closed door, clothes rustling. My knuckles paused over the wood in my hesitation to knock. Part of me wanted to interrupt her and break the spell that seemed to have befallen all of us, but the other part wanted what she was freely about to get.

By the time I'd made up my mind to knock, it was too late. I heard the blunt shove of bodies thrusting awkwardly against the door, then the unmistakable sound of groaned lust followed by a female catlike yowl of hungry passion.

Their pounding rhythm against the wood became harder, and I closed my eyes, my hand unfurling to press against the door as if to seek its pulse.

How long I stood there, I don't know, but I was suddenly aware that the crescendo was coming and that someone stood at my back, so close that I could smell the leather and musk from him.

My eyes popped open as he aligned completely behind me; thighs behind mine, feet beside mine, one hand next to where mine braced on the door frame, the other covering my hand where I was feeling the activity on the door.

"Brad," I whispered, temporarily unable to do anything less than return his provocative grind with my buttocks. He groaned as one of his large hands moved to clasp a breast while curving his rock-hard cock once more against me.

"Estelle..." His lips barely grazed my neck and my knees threatened to give in. On the other side of the door, the thuds crested with a coarse masculine shout, and I found myself trembling.

Brad's right hand moved over the shiver of my naked belly, down into my low-slung hip skirt and plunged between my parted thighs, right into my wetness as if he had every right to.

"Yes!" I barely whispered as he simultaneously rubbed his groin against my buttocks. Again the fingers slid over my clitoris in that mindless, perfect, circular-plunge motion, rubbing, stroking...

The sounds of voices behind the door jarred me into reality. I heard a belt buckle and realized they were getting ready to step out of the room.

"No!" I whispered in harsh panic as I blindly pulled his hand away from my undies. After a brief shocked moment, I watched in a half-mesmerized state as he lifted my wetness to his nose and inhaled my scents. At his quiet hum of approval, I took another stumbling step back.

There was more movement behind the door, enough to make me turn around and escape into the garden.

Outside a full moon glowed, and I felt possessed by its flawless light. My body burned from within, my mind fixed on the sole yearning of my vagina, my nipples, my panting mouth. I ran past rosebushes, a Koi pond and finally the gardening shed, the jingle of my cloak marking my passage. I finally stopped at

24

the farthest corner of the yard, leaning against the trunk of a curved pine tree.

I waited for the cold to return me to normal, but my body ached from my inner furnace. What was I doing? Why did I want to run back in there and let him continue where we had left off? For heaven's sakes, we weren't even friends!

At the distance I could hear the sensuous tune that followed the nightclub jazz sounds. Then like an invader in the night, I suddenly heard Brad approaching, his spurs marking the narrowing distance. I straightened my shoulders, determined not to let my hormones get the best of me this time.

He came to stand closer, broad-shouldered and legs apart, as if he expected to tackle me. Still, he stood much too close for what was comfortable, yet far enough that I could make a run for it.

"You and I have unfinished business," he growled. I could see he was quite obviously aroused but still festering with anger and unclaimed passion. He leaned his hands by my face, blocking off any possible retreat.

"Can't take no for an answer?" I taunted.

"Ah," he said more softly, "but you said yes first."

We glared at each other for several moments. I swallowed nervously, noisily, unable to deny that I still wanted to scream yes all over again. He brought his head closer, and I felt his warm breath chasing the cold wind from my cheek. "Tell me no right now and I'll stop."

I shivered, my hands gripping the bark at my spine. "Look, I think this has gone far enough"

"That doesn't sound like a no."

"I don't see the purpose of..."

He made a disapproving sound. "You and me, Estelle. We've been sniffing and snarling at each other for months, like animals in heat. God knows why, but I want you. You've been twitching in my system, driving me crazy.... I know about all those not-so-nice things you say about me at work and, hell, I've said some stuff about you, too, but the truth between us is this, isn't it?"

"You're nuts."

"Am I?"

"You're jealous because I landed the Knodel account."

He chuckled, the sound, warm and mischievous, and more than a bit sexy. "Woman, you're in denial if you think I'm here because of some account."

I refused to respond, because I knew I was grasping at straws.

He was so close now that I could see the humor leave his eyes and his pupils become depths of the darkest brown. His voice was calm with confident seduction. "Have you ever touched yourself, touched that hot, slippery wetness, and imagined that your fingers are mine...masturbating while thinking about us getting it on, working up a sweat, humping? Do you ever imagine how it would feel to have me deep inside you?"

Even without my outraged gasp, he must have read the truth in my eyes. His grin widened. "I do. I think of you when I'm stroking myself, imagining your lovely thighs, parted, with your wet center, ready for tasting. I've been wanting to hear you say my name the way I know it should sound and not the way you like to bark it over the phone at work. I want to memorize the sound of your voice when I'm deep inside you, giving you all I've got. I can't wait to hear your breath when you cum."

I couldn't speak. I couldn't even breathe. I just stood there, mute and burning while his lips landed butterfly kisses on my jaw.

"You're such an enigma. Dressing like a flirt and behaving like you're frigid. But I'd bet my last dollar that you're a firecracker, honey."

I inhaled sharply. "You'd go broke."

"I don't think so. You've got about three more seconds to say no," he whispered in my ear, his words breathless and urgent. Despite the obvious seduction, I knew he was giving me a way out.

Already his hand was curving up my ribcage and I bit my lip to hold back a moan. I should put him in his place. Tell him to back off. Say that simple word no.

"Three." His teeth sank a soft pain into my arched neck. A love bite.

"Two." His wide palms cupped my breasts. But not the nipples.

"One." His body was flush against mine in full-body contact, setting off the soft sound of the tiny bells and coins of my cloak. The moan I'd been holding back escaped, and I moved my hips involuntarily where his crotch nudged into mine.

"Tell me you want me, honey," he murmured. "There's no shame in it."

I finally nodded, managing to say, "Yes," but my word came out like a soft plea. Dangerous or not, I wanted him! If I was a firecracker, I wanted him to be the one to prove it.

He kissed me hard, his mouth crushing mine in a thoroughly possessive kiss that robbed me of breath. His lips, tongue and mouth licked, sucked and swallowed me, devouring my mouth like a man who'd been waiting a long time to taste this particular meal. His hands roamed over me and the cloak was pushed back when it hindered his exploration.

Cool night air touched my naked skin like ice water, but Brad's touch chased away the chill, leaving a tingling trail that brought shivers of another kind.

The far-off music sped like the gallop of a wild herd, spiraling into the air like the calls from minarets. In his arms, the chime of tiny cymbals and bells shimmered as I eased against him.

"Let me show you how to make music for me," he whispered, his open palms barely cresting my breasts. The static of his touch shimmied through me, giving him what he wanted, a sultry, inviting sound of music in my groan and my cloak. I kissed him with a mixed rush of victory and surrender. I felt starved, hungry, taking mouthfuls of kisses while feeling the bristle of his jaw under my palms.

And even as we moved in the foreplay of the age-old sexual dance, our needs pushed us into an edge of desperation.

"Stelle," he moaned when his hands slipped under my harem top, the weight of my full breasts slipping into his palms. His touch was delightfully hot as his hands moved over my nipples, so hot it burned into me.

"Please," I begged.

He thrust his hips against mine, knowing my need and still depriving me of it. "Say my name," he ordered as he licked the base of my ear then nibbled on my lobe.

"Brad."

"Again."

"No," I rebelled, turning my head and finding the pulse point on his neck, nibbling then kissing the saltiness from his skin. He reacted just as I had.

"What's my name?" I dared to ask, barely brave.

His fingers worked off my bra. "You're...mine," he said triumphantly before cupping my breasts and pushing them gently together. He buried his face in my cleavage, his mouth sucking on my breasts and my nipples until I was groaning again.

The telltale chime of the cloak revealed my pleasure almost as much as my whimpers, but when I moved a trembling hand to remove the noisy garment, he stopped me.

"Keep it on." The request was murmured just before his mouth found mine again until finally, his lips went on to discover the vulnerability of my nape. His hands gathered the translucent folds of silk that had made up my skirt, cupping my buttocks and pulling me even more against him. My fingers worked feverishly to undo his shirt, and finally, I could feel his naked chest touching mine. The light sprinkling of his chest hair was incredibly sensual on my nipples. Thick with need, his sex pushed against my damp apex, and the bells sang softly.

"Open," he commanded.

His breath filled my lungs as if I'd been running, filling me with the smells of him, the sounds of seductive drums and the race of my quaking pulse. I felt flushed, mortified with the guilt of pleasure, as I allowed him to ease my legs apart. With his eyes locked on me, he undid his jeans and a moment later, I felt his hands against my juncture, gathering my moisture and using his fingers to lubricate my labia and clitoris with it.

"Christ... Please!" I begged.

"My name," he said in a rough whisper, his fingers still waiting to penetrate.

"Brad..." His fingers plunged into me, experimentally at first, then deeper as carnality drove my hips to meet his hand.

"Silk," he said with a fierce satisfaction. "Hmm, yes..."

The cloak revealed my need for his fingers. Easing to a faster beat, I clung to his brawny shoulders and rode his fingers until I could feel a zenith arising behind my eyes. Then without warning he suddenly withdrew his hand, leaving me greedy and bereft.

"Hold on, Estelle." The heat of his sex was quickly sheathed in a condom then, hard and eager, it pressed against the wet lips of my slit.

"Music. I want to hear your music...feel it," he whispered as he penetrated me, deeply, thoroughly, holding me so that I cried out and arched away from the tree trunk to accommodate his possession.

"Shhh, easy honey," he whispered, kissing me tenderly, his voice sounding as if he was in agony. "Relax. Relax and take all of me."

With eyes tightly shut, I focused on the delight of his lips on my breasts, his hands lifting me up just enough to then lower me unto his cob again until the tightness began to abate.

And so the rhythm began. Pure music.

The dance was a cresting thrust, an overwhelming penetration, then a succulent withdrawal that caused trembling on my inner thighs. I had never felt so connected before, so deeply, so physically in tune with all the other emotions bombarding me. I could barely believe that the muffled song of occasional moans and inhibited whimpers were mine.

Even our breathing added a unique tempo, inhaling, exhaling jaggedly, sometimes paused by the force of our kisses. The clinks and shimmers of the cloak bells were accompanied by the far off drums and tambourines.

"Oh, my God," I whispered, feeling my world start to spin off a whirling fulcrum. "Oh...Oh!...Brad!"

"Come," he coaxed, his bristly jaw scraping my neck, his teeth punishing my throat, perspiration mixing with mine against my cheek. "Come..."

It was inevitable, I realized with surprise, I was going to...

The impact of his next thrust sent me over the edge, over color and sound, into a place where I was completely undone. My eyes flew open at the sudden wave of rushing within me, strong enough to make my womb quiver and my ears ring with the chimes of the shaking cloak. My second cry burst out of me like a startled bird. Through my blurred vision, I saw his face, fierce with restraint, his eyes hot black.

"Beautiful," his words were deep and rough and husky, barely reaching my ears. The tremor of his muscles told me he was about to succumb and so I tried to tightened my vaginal muscles and delighted in feeling his control stripping until he moved wildly into me, bucking hard like a fevered bronco, in racking thrusts that shoved me roughly against the tree. I felt delirious, whimpering from the thorough lubricated plundering. As the force of his thrusts reached a peak, he grunted, releasing his hot semen deep into my womb.

Even then, I trembled at the thrill of it, and I held on as the shudders kept me impaled against the tree, filling the night with the long crescendo of tiny chimes.

Several long moments later, still joined, he lifted his head from where he'd buried it against my neck. Without words we kissed again, leisurely and with such an intimacy I felt I'd never, ever been kissed before.

"Boy," I finally said.

He smiled, revealing his handsome dimple. "You sure do make beautiful music."

I chuckled and clung to him as if it was the most natural thing in the world. But already reality was starting to intrude.

"I hope you don't think this changes our working relationship," I lied, making it sound like an afterthought.

His right hand cupped and weighed my breast. Deep in me, I could feel his erection stirring back to life.

"Brad," I warned, but he was already grinning, lowering his head to kiss me.

"We'll see," was all he said before starting the strains of a new song that shimmered over my cloak. "Now, about that mouth organ..."

Masquerade (Tasha's story)

The night was young, the music was hot and here I was, dressed like a French maid in the middle of a Halloween party sponsored by my job. I'll admit, I'd been looking forward to this, wondering what people would wear, wondering how loose and bold the alcohol would make my coworkers.

As for me, I was really getting into my role. Maybe the outfit was a tad too tight, but that worked to my benefit. Heck, my small breasts didn't look so small thanks to this pushup bra that made a hell of a display rack of my twins. Looking in the ladies' room mirror, I used some blush, trailing the brush over them and noticing how they looked like two round rolls of bread, baked to brown perfection and nestled in the basket that was the white halter top. Warm and yummy for the right guy.

I frowned at the black skirt though. Somehow between the time I left my house and the first dance, I swear this thing shrank a bit. Good thing I work out and my legs look good. At least I'd like to think they are my best feature.

This skirt was already so short, that if I bent the wrong way, anyone could get a pretty close glimpse of my mother nature. I stood, realizing the garters were probably making peek-a-boos as I walked. Damn.

I tried walking around, which made the few ruffles of the skirt fluff out sassily. Providing easy access, as my ex-boyfriend would say. That creep.

Tonight was mine.

There was no room in my mind for that jerk this evening. I planned on strutting my fishnet legs all over the dance floor, getting my groove on and then...really getting my groove, if you know what I mean. I've had it with expectations, polite conversations and men who treat my body like a plastic blow-up doll.

My passionate affair with my new BOB (battery-operated-boyfriend) was great but still lacked the full-body contact I desired. Tonight I wanted my own boy toy for a change correction, I want me a man toy.

With one last check of my makeup, I winked at my reflection for luck and headed out the door.

The music was loud enough for me to pretend to be deaf to the dances I didn't want and accept the ones that I did.

The Wolfman from accounting bought me a martini, the hairy-chested pirate from personnel kept buying me screwdrivers, and a bleeding surgeon tried to give me a Bloody Mary. I was getting tipsy, but not drunk enough to settle for any of these guys. And the dancing was making me hot, making the fishnets and garters feel sensuous on my legs, making the sheen of perspiration glow on my twins and making me quite hungry for sex.

It was while I was dancing to a slower groove that I shut my eyes for just a few moments, and when I opened them, I found myself dancing with a Rastafarian vampire. The man was almost as dark as his cloak, with intelligent eyes and a mysterious smile.

It was cool that he didn't try to make conversation like the other guys. Instead he came up close, dancing with me nice and slow, sometimes letting his body touch me, and other times letting me touch him. I loved that cocky lift of his smile, the unspoken communication in his eyes, the way he was making me feel sexy and wicked, like I had no idea the delights I was in for. He looked familiar, but I didn't want to know just yet who he was or where he worked in the company.

Over the speakers, Anita Baker was crooning like a mellow saxophone, and the husky tone slipped softly over me, giving a more decadent twist to the evening, to how I was feeling. When the song ended, I went back to the bar, aware that my vampire was following.

"Hey, Dracula," the bartender greeted as if they knew each other.

Dracula waved and sidled up next to me. "Hi, Cedric. Would you mind if I made the lady a drink?"

Ohhh, an accent! Not the fake Dracula talk, but a genuine something with a touch of Latin. Or was that French?

"Nice accent," I commented. In the weak light and with the contrast of his dark suit, the flash of his slow bright smile was seductive.

"Be back in a moment," was all he said, then moved on behind the bar. I watched his steady walk, wishing his cape wouldn't hide the shape of his butt or the width of his back. I was considering his potential for my man-toy pursuit when I noticed he was watching me in the mirror. His gaze was steady, his low-key chuckle too knowing, so I turned away to check out the crowd.

Half an eternity later, I saw a crystal champagne flute slipped next to my fingers as I turned back to the bar.

"Your drink, my lady." The shade of pink was unusual, with the sunlight gold of champagne and the ruby red of cranberry juice. At the bottom were a few pomegranate seeds and on the top he'd floated tiny red petals, like the edible ones that had been in our buffet salad.

I took a cautious sip and made an appreciative sound when the flavor revealed juice and wine. Except I think the juice was grenadine instead of cranberry. "Delicious. What do you call it?"

"Love Potion Number Two."

"Really? Whatever happened to Love Potion Number One?"

"That aphrodisiac was mine."

The cool liquid slipped down my throat as he held my gaze. It trailed down cool but became warm as it descended farther, until I could feel the wetness curl into the yearning in my gut, coming lower still to where my legs were crossed. If he were next to me, I would've let him sink his teeth into my neck without much of a complaint.

"Aphrodisiac? Interesting. I've had my share of alcohol tonight. What makes you think this drink will make any difference?" I asked.

Again that slow smile appeared. "Because the drink was made for you, just like the other one was made for me." The deep rumble and the slight accent worked to speed up my pulse. He raised the glass to my lips, and I took another sip. I know all about the power of suggestion, but quite suddenly I indulged in the illusion that I really was drinking an aphrodisiac, that he had, too, and that soon we'd both have to do something about it.

"How do you like it?" he asked.

Several ways, really. On my back. Against the wall. On my knees. "I'm still thinking about it," I replied, pretending I was thinking about the drink, but the depths of his eyes warmed as if I'd revealed my thoughts.

Feeling a bit nervous, I took a longer sip, then licked my lips. He reached out and ran his thumb over my bottom lip, trailing the moisture there. I felt breathless, and with a boldness I didn't usually have in public, I licked the pad of his thumb before sinking my teeth delicately into his finger. Then I licked the soft pain I'd induced and sucked gently on the bite marks.

His smile faded and the heat in his eye blazed. His handsome face was taut with want, his nostrils flared, and I felt as if there was no one else in the room but the two of us.

"Dance with me," he murmured, and I knew he meant it in more than the obvious innuendo. This was it, I decided. This man was going to be my sexual relief, my man toy and I was going to work him until I was weak and satisfied.

"Let's go," I replied.

He walked around and pulled me onto the crowded dance floor. What we did had little to do with dancing and more to do with testing the waters, or better said, testing the fires. We moved together, doing the dance of clothed lovers, touching and aligning our hips so the tempo was a constant timer. Our movements revealed just how hard his erection was for me. His hands moved on my hips and back, and every once in a while, he'd lean forward and murmur some lyrics in my ear in his deep voice.

"...I'll take you to the moon, taste the flower of your bloom, make you tremble like a butterfly..."

I felt his knee nudge between my legs, and we worked that into an interesting move. "Promises, promises," I mocked a bit breathlessly.

"...no rules, no denials, tonight I will create fires, all for you and your desires..."

This time when we turned, he stalled and held me so I rode his thigh for just a fraction of a moment longer. I clutched his shoulders and let him do it to me again. The chemistry between us was so volatile, I could feel the invisible sparks. I realized I was feeling quite sober, but also insanely aroused. Maybe there had been something in the Love Potion Number Two after all.

He took my hand in his firm grip and led me off the dance floor to an isolated corner, then proceeded to kiss me as if he'd been too long denied. It was a slow, languid kiss but powerfully erotic lips, tongue and hungry mouth. His hands roamed to my hips where he held me to his erection, letting me feel the thickness until I wanted to squirm against it.

After a few breathless moments, his hands moved to my breasts, cupping the small weight in his hands and grazing his thumbs over my sensitive nipples.

"Oh yesssss," I moaned as I arched my back, wanting his mouth on them. Instead his hand boldly slipped down my belly, under the skirt until the tips of his fingers touched my pubic hair.

I heard a shimmer, like chimes and felt his muscles tense. Gasping, I looked over his shoulder and spotted a woman dressed like a genie. Or maybe she was a harem dancer, I don't know. The flute she was holding on to threw me off. But what had alerted us was the tiny bells and coins sewn on to the edge of her cape. I was suddenly embarrassed and tried to shrink into his chest.

"How about a little privacy?" I whispered sternly to Dracula.

"Absolutely." Oh yeah, I could hear the French in that word.

Without a backward glimpse at the woman, we left. I followed blindly while Dracula's cape billowed and his steps lengthened. He led me past the dancers, past other guests, down a hall where he began to test the doorknobs. Some were locked but he found one open.

"Here," he said, already leading me into the dark chamber. It was a large bedroom with a tall ceiling and lots of windows on one side. In the center, a huge bed invited while on the side, an Oriental screen offered extra privacy. I was amazed to see a small cage with a live monkey sitting in it. The monkey was beige and small, like the one with the organgrinder at the fair. It stared at us with a startled expression then bared his teeth nervously.

Other large pieces of furniture were revealed in the moonlight but we stood on the spot, unable to decide where to go first. The decision was taken from our hands when we heard laughter and footsteps coming from down the hall.

"Quick, the screen!" he said, tugging me behind the three Oriental panels. We'd barely slipped behind when a Caucasian couple stumbled into the room, going right for the bed. It was the host and his wife! They'd been the only ones to dress like President Clinton and Monica Lewinsky, although neither of them really pulled it off.

I bent to peer between the folds of the screen, watching. They were like animals, stumbling on the bed, ripping at clothes and finally removing enough for sex. In the ruckus, Monica's wig flew through the air, knocking down the monkey cage from its precarious spot with a loud bang. There was a loud screech followed by a shadowy leap as the little monkey escaped the cage and bounced around the room, chattering nervously.

"Shit!" Bill grumbled.

"Forget him! He's harmless, just"

"Give you this?" His erection arched out, shorter but thicker than I'd ever seen. He parted her milky-white thighs, and placed his poised-and-ready erection at the juncture of her thighs.

"Yes!"

He thrust in, and she gripped the sheets, arching her back and crying out softly. "Ahhhh, yes, baby!"

The monkey leapt twice, bouncing off the bedpost, then a sconce until he swung from the crystal chandelier above the bed, causing a pendulum effect as it hung on to the frame.

I covered my mouth to keep from laughing, turning to see if Dracula had noticed. When I looked over my shoulder, I saw that he was busy rolling on a condom over his thick, rock-hard penis. Some of his dreds had fallen forward on his cape and the filtering moonlight gave his eyes a haunting, sexy look.

He reached to lift my skirt, the slight sounds mixing with the moans and grunts of the couple on the bed. I could hear the slight squeak of the chandelier as it swayed, but everything in my being concentrated on the feel of his strong fingers as they parted my legs, unclipped the crotch of my panties and slipped his fingers into my slippery cunt.

Holy ssssmoke! I gasped then bit my lip hard to squelch any sound as I rode the incredibly delicious sensation of invading digits. He plunged in again and I worked my Kegel muscles to grip his fingers. I made a desperate grab for his cape and covered my mouth with it, muffling another need to groan. This was the hardest torture! He moved so slowly, rubbing with pressure, rimmed my sensitive nub in an expert touch, plunging and grazing my wetness until I rocked against his hand.

As quickly as the other lovers were bouncing on the mattress, Dracula was taking his sweet time on me. All the way from my toes to the back of my spine, my legs quivered, waiting and bracing for each slow dive of his hand. Bent over the way I was, my nipples brushed against the very top edge of my barmaid top, and I'd never realized how sensually scratchy that material could get.

I looked back, trying to let him understand the urgency in me, of how close I was to making noises. He reached for my arm, pulling it toward him until he had my hand against the heat of his cock. Singlehandedly, I rubbed his erection, enjoying the thickness of it in my grip then slipping my hands lower to cup his testicles.

It was sweet to hear his hiss of breath, to see him close his eyes and fight for control. I allowed him to move my hand away and felt him prepare to plunge into me. I looked straight ahead and waited.

On the bed, Monica had flipped Bill on his back and was riding him like a cowgirl on a wild mustang. I could see the graphic penetration, could hear the wetness of their surges and merges mingling with their loud panting. I could even smell them.

I was watching this when Dracula began to push his big, blunt cock into me. I couldn't hold back a whimper as the inches grew, pushing deeper until he was fully lodged deep inside.

With his large palms on my ass, he withdrew just as slowly and re-entered at the same pace.

"Ommph!" My gagged cry was lost in the midst of the other sounds. I tried closing my eyes, but that only intensified each ripple of movement, and when my eyes were opened, I had a full view of the sex on the sheets, which was just as effective. In and out, I suffered the insanely slow pleasure, my lungs straining to give voice to the thrills.

I could feel my body already tightening, bracing for the impact of the orgasm that threatened to rip through me. He stopped thrusting to curl against my spine, one of his hands going to stroke my clitoris while the other released my breasts from their confines. Even in his hands, my breasts felt big and so very sensitive.

We remained in that position, without motion. And even then, I didn't think I'd be able to withstand much more of the intensity. It just felt so real, so hard, so sexy to not move at all. Then the semi-rough touch of his calluses had my nipples at tight peaks. I clenched my vaginal muscles and heard him grind his teeth, his harsh breathing feeling hot against my ear.

He whispered something foreign and urgent, thrusting slow and hard into me while simultaneously stroking my clitoris between his fingers. It was as if I'd surfed right off a roaring wave.

The orgasm hit me like a series of abdominal hiccups, and I was helpless to do anything more than inhale through my nose, biting down on the cape that muffled my sounds, while my body came undone. I know I had his cape like a gag in my mouth, but I'm not even sure it was lack of oxygen that made me feel like I was about to faint.

I felt his arms tighten around me, felt the softness of his hair dropping on my neck as he bit softly into my nape to keep from howling out his own release. With the tiniest of thrusts I felt him cum and felt the shake of his body on mine.

We remained there, catching our breath as quietly as possible while the lovers in bed were easing out of their grunts, murmuring love nothings to each other. He then raised his cape, covering us. I think he did this to muffle our breathing.

All I know is that I finally heard the couple adjust their clothes and leave the room, the smell of sex remaining in the air.

From the chandelier, the little monkey chattered while observing us, and Dracula and I reluctantly separated. He adjusted his clothes but brushed my hands aside when I went to straighten mine.

"Allow me," he said as he clipped the crotch of my underwear back into place. I saw the first traces of his slow smile before he bent his head and lavished oral attention to my breasts. I clutched his coarse-soft hair, amazed that I could feel tremors of arousal so soon.

Eventually, he placed lingering kisses on my nipples and tugged the shirt back into place.

"Come home with me," he coaxed, not really looking at me. When he finally made eye contact he said, "There is so much more I want to show you."

I hesitated, not wanting the experience to evolve into something more tangible.

"I can practically hear your wheels turning," he said as a smile played on his lips and accent. "You don't know who I am and you'd like to keep it that way, right?"

Well, since he was being blunt... "Yes."

He nodded. "You can trust me. I can even blindfold you if you'd like so you won't know where I live. Just for tonight."

"Hmmm. And when morning comes?"

"I'll take you home. No questions asked. No demands."

I played with a strand of his hair. "So, you want to be my man toy, huh?"

He chuckled, the sound like velvet. "I suppose. What I really want is to explore all of you, to take my time doing so."

I smiled, feeling the thrill of his words and the promise in the hushed, accented voice. "We weren't exactly hurrying a few minutes ago."

"We can go slower, draw it out longer."

Oh, my! I wondered briefly if he was messing with my mind, but he seemed so arrogantly confident, so eager to prove it to me. The offer was entirely too tempting to pass up.

I smiled. "Okay, let's go."

Masquerade (Tina's story)

I couldn't decide what to wear to my roommate's Halloween party, so I thought I'd cover two issues with one call.

Issue one, of course, was what to wear and issue two was the booty call (or as I call it BC). I checked out my hot-pink nail polish as I picked up the phone and dialed.

Let me explain about the BC, though. Jeff and I have had this agreement for about a year now. I call him and he gives it up and vice versa. There's nothing better when you don't want complications! I was through with getting lines like "Hey, are you gonna break me off a little sum'thin'-sum'thin'?" From some STD stud, or worse yet, getting stuck with a man who wants to spend the night getting in touch with his feminine side.

Puhleeez! BC keeps it real, you know?

I could hear the phone ring until finally it was picked up on the third time. A deep voice answered, a bit impatiently. "Hello."

"Hey, it's me," I said. No need to ID myself.

"Hey, you." The smooth tone of his voice became warm, saying it all. "I'm so glad you called."

"Really? Did I catch you at a bad time?"

I heard the rustling of paper and what sounded like a binder slamming shut. "Nope," he said, sighing as if I'd made his day. "Just more casework."

Jeff was a lawyer. A damned good one too. As a matter of fact, his brain turned me on almost as much as his body. "Wanna go to a Halloween party?"

"Oh...yeah, sounds good." I could tell he was a bit disappointed.

"Cheer up," I said, making it sound like a reprimand. "It's still a BC. Just not at your house."

"Hold on," he said, but I could hear the smile in his voice. "Isn't it my turn this time?"

I laughed. "You know good and well who's turn it is! Nice try though."

He laughed, loud and full of vigor, the sound coming across the wires to embrace me.

"So? You wanna go?"

"Sure. You don't have restaurant duty tonight?"

My sisters and I own a restaurant, the Soul Food Soufflé, but I'd told them days before that I was leaving early. Two of us are chefs but my other sister is always trying to get out of doing the cleaning.

"No scrub duty tonight," I replied. "Do you think you can find something for the party?"

I could hear him rustling about. "Umm, well, I could be a cowboy-"

"Nuh-uh."

"Well, then, I've got these leather pants, a leather vest and an eyepatch."

"Sounds interesting."

"A pirate costume?"

"Hmm." I'm guessing there are going to be plenty of those.

"The Terminator?"

"I'm liking that.... Tell me more...."

"How about the Ejaculator?"

I chuckled. "What?"

"The Human Vibrator?"

I laughed. "You planning on wearing a condom over your head?"

His reply was warped and I could tell he was going through his closet trying to hold the phone with his shoulder. "That depends on which head you're talking about. Speaking of which... Should I bring the jelly rolls?"

Jelly rolls are special flavored condoms. My favorite was peppermint.

42

Cinnamon was delicious too. I once tried banana, which by the way, also glows in the dark, but yuck, it tasted like feet smell. "Yeah, bring the rolls. You know the ones."

"You got it. Anything else?"

I gave him directions to the party, adding, "I sure hope you're nice and rested. I've got plans for you."

* * *

This party was the bomb! I'd lost my roommate in the crowd but we'd agreed to meet each other at home anyway.

"Rah-rah, little girl," this guy said as he came up next to me. I think he was supposed to be Elvis, but he had a blue cape with butterflies on it and I couldn't figure out why.

"Hey, Elvis," I replied, my arms already tired from carrying my pom-poms around. I was feeling good in my high school cheerleading outfit. I still hadn't grown an inch over five foot two since back in the day, and my curves did tighten the seams a bit, but it fit.

Okay, so I had to adjust the top a little bit, which made my large breasts look like a brown baby's butt, ready to spill out. The bright red and white announced I was an Edgar Hoover High School cheerleader. The logo had brought about a couple of leers and wiggled fingers in my direction: The Trojans!

And as our cheer went, "Say it loud, say it proud...Troooojans!"

Elvis was giving me the eye, and when he smiled, I caught the glimpse of his gold tooth. "If you do a cheer for me I'll buy you a drink."

From behind me, I heard, "The lady is with me."

Sure enough, I turned around and saw Jeff. Or should I say, The Terminator. He was looking tough in the leather outfit he'd talked about. His arms and chest were ripped, showing off all his fine, hard muscles. The sides of his head were shaved and shiny, and he'd combed up the tight afro at the top. He had on some gunmetal black shades and wore a series of plastic bullets like a weapon across his chest.

I turned in time to notice that Elvis had become a bit nervous. He curled up his lip, said "Uh-huh" and moved on.

Jeff relaxed, smiled at me, obviously having enjoyed his role of being a macho jock. I couldn't help it, I put down one of my pom-poms and reached over to squeeze the hard muscles of his arm. Nice. Oooh, so nice!

"You're such a macho stud!" I said, using my fake cheerleader voice.

Jeff flagged the bartender as if he was used to women squeezing him all the time. "Listen," he said, lowering his shades just a bit so we could really look at each other. Wiggling his eyebrows, he said, "If I buy you a drink, will you do a cheer for me?"

The way he said it sent a thrill down my spine, unlike the first time I heard the words. "Oh yeah...Want me to do the splits for you?"

He licked his full lips and his voice lowered. "I'm sorry, I don't think I heard you, you know with the music and all. Did you say for me or on me?"

The bartender interrupted and I was saved from a reply, but that little comment made me get all hot.

Someone turned the music up even higher and unfortunately a group of people came over next to us, which pushed me against Jeff. The drinks came and I was shoved again, practically putting me in Jeff's lap.

So maybe that wasn't bad, since my ass was now on his crotch. I gave him an accidental bump and got a come-on from his penis. A rub, rub, grind got me a warning growl in my ear.

"Wanna dance?" I asked innocently when his arm grabbed my waist.

"Sure." But his eyes warned me I was going to pay for flirting like that.

The speakers were thumping old eighties hits, so we worked up a sweat to Bobby Brown's "My Prerogative". I love to watch Jeff move. He's tall, black and sure looks dangerous. He doesn't always get the moves right, but when he's got it going on, it's almost hypnotic.

He brushed up against me, while his eyes remained glued to the jiggle of my breasts. I turned around and he pushed up against me again, letting me feel his erection like a steel pipe in his leather pants.

Very, very nice!

My breasts felt tingly, my kitten was achy and my mouth was thirsty for Jeff's. I turned around again, grabbed him by his vest and leaned up to talk into his ear. "We need to find a BC suite now."

There was no hesitation whatsoever. Just a huge grin and his, "Come on then."

We made it off the dance floor, then Jeff led the way through one of the halls. We tried a few knobs, but the doors were locked. Finally one opened and we rushed inside.

I barely caught a glimpse of an office when Jeff pushed me up against the wall and began to kiss me hard and hungry.

Remember how I said the man can't dance? Well, he sure as hell can kiss! I mean, really kiss. Like the way I used to neck back in high school. That mouth of his just gobbles me up until I can't add up two simple numbers.

"What jelly roll do you want?" he asked, his breath all ragged, like he'd been running.

"Peppermint."

I reached under my skirt, between my legs and tugged at the delicate lace undies until it ripped. I saw him reach into one of the bullet slots and pull out a white condom. Within seconds he'd unzipped his leather pants and was rolling it on. I reached for it eagerly, grabbing the thick meat and stroking it gently.

Jeff moaned low "Oh, babe...hold up...wait... "

He moved my hands to his shoulders, but I was already feeling the peppermint tingle on my hands. Without any effort, he grabbed me by the ass, lifted me and began to push his lovely cock into my wet ache.

"Oooh, that's good," I moaned, feeling his peppermint penis slide deep inside. I wiggled, settling deeper and feeling the effects of peppermint start to work.

"Slow or fast," he asked as he got ready to shove in again.

"Fast. Oh yes, please!"

He was on it, picking up pace and ramming into me until our bodies were bumping against the door. I didn't even think about it twice. All I knew was that peppermint pipe felt hot and cold inside me every time he plugged away. Suckalicious! Delicious! It felt so damn good!

"Oh, yeah, baby," he said between groans, and I could feel his cock getting even bigger inside me. He kissed me breathless until I almost saw stars. I could feel and hear the wet and juicy friction. That thickening penis seemed to nudge clear into my gut, making me squirm to take more, to feel more, until I suddenly lost it, crying out and holding on to him while he still moved in and out.

"Oh my. Oh my...God!" He shoved me hard against the door, a full-body bump and grind that ended in a shudder, squeezing off his orgasm deep inside me.

"Jeffreeey!"

"Oh!" He breathed, swallowing dryly before gasping again. "Oh my God...I think I'm going to pass out."

I weakly glanced at him, worried he might be serious, but he was grinning. "Okay, I lied. But I do need to lay down just a bit."

Separating was another sensitive experience altogether. Jeff rested with his back to the floor. I leaned back on the executive desk and waited for the heat, breathlessness and dizziness to stop.

We lay there for quite a while until I heard him move again. I felt him kneel between my thighs, his lips on my vaginal ones. His hot mouth started to lick up the mixture of peppermint and cum.

"Ooh, Jeff. Jeff!"

"Girl, you know I like peppermint." His tongue was slick, tricky and wild, licking me with skill. "You taste so good, baby."

"Shh. Don't stop."

He chuckled but kept his mouth on me. I know it was more than ten minutes that I lay there, squirming and begging while he ate me up. At some point, I unbuttoned my top, showing him the tiny red-and-white pasties I'd glued to my nipples.

His tongue slowed down, so I knew he was watching me. I touched my breasts and wiggled them a bit, making the tassels shake.

"Sing it," he said, taking a small nibble of my inner thigh.

I was breathing hard, but I went for it, doing my cheer in my sexiest singsong voice. "We are the Trooojans and no one could be prouder. And if you don't believe us, we'll yell a little louuuder."

His mouth stopped altogether. I lowered one hand and began to masturbate, knowing he would try to watch my breasts and my clit.

"Oh yeaaaah," he grunted, already licking between my fingers as I dipped inside myself.

"Hurry. I can't wait," I said, feeling the grip of pleasure start in my gut.

"Okay." But he kept licking my clit and fingers even as he put on another condom.

Ooh, cinnamon! I could smell it.

"Now. Now!"

And there he was, sliding into me smooth, deep and...Lord Almighty, that felt good! I could feel and smell peppermint and cinnamon, and when he kissed me, I could taste all that and sex. Like we had mixed sex and cooking and eating all at the same time.

Delicious!

It took only two shoves for me to lose it, crying out and gripping him hard with my legs to keep him inside me.

Right after that, he grunted loudly, shoved me so hard that the desk moved, and came like a pistol.

We lay there sweating for a while, and when he grabbed my breasts to kiss them, the pasties slid right off.

"Wow," I said as we stood to fix ourselves. "You were like the Terminator!"

He leaned against the desk and I could tell he was a bit tuckered out. "Yeah?"

"Wait, you were more like the Ejaculator or the Human Vibrator."

He slapped me on the butt, teasingly. "And that would make you what? The Orgazmicator."

I smiled coyly. "Yeahhhh."

Grocery Shopping

"Cleanup on aisle three!" the overhead speaker barked. A young worker moved past me, a mop in his grasp as if it was a gladiator's spear.

I continued pushing my cart down the frozen-food aisle and paused to check on ice cream. Mmm, strawberry, my husband's favorite. Then pistachio, my favorite! I popped my gum as I gave the indecision two seconds of thought. My husband, the inconsiderate, unthinking fool, was most definitely in the dog-house, therefore the ice cream choice was really a no-brainer. I mean, I understand he's a businessman and all, and that he had to travel most of the time, but I hadn't seen him in almost a month! He was supposed to come home today.

But instead he canceled our anniversary dinner.

Still, I sighed and deliberated some more with the door open, wondering if my hips could handle much more decadence. Reluctantly, I closed the door, catching not only my own frowning reflection but that of a man down the aisle, his gaze fixed intently on me. The glass door began to shut and the semi-familiar image disappeared, but now I was too wary to even turn around.

Me? He was looking at me? Maybe that pistachio ice cream deserved another look. As casually as possible, I opened the door, and checked the reflection for the man again. To my disappointment, the aisle was now clear of any traffic. I turned to check. Gone.

How odd. There had been something sexy in the way he'd been watching me.

I dumped the bucket of my husband's favorite ice cream into my shopping cart, then reminded myself that I could have been dining at the Hyatt if only he hadn't canceled!

The tap-tap-tap made me realize I was drumming my fingers in annoyance. Which also reminded me that I had wasted my time and money getting the perfect manicure just hours ago. I had gone through all that trouble just to impress my man during dinner. My husband likes nails that scratch and leave small marks on him, and I was planning to show him.

The bastard.

I paused by the frozen pizzas wondering if I should get one. I settled for the pepperoni and was about to close the door when someone moved in from behind me, slipping his hand in and grabbing a box for himself.

"Oh, pardon me," he said quietly, his gaze remaining on mine a few seconds beyond what was considered cordial. It was him! I sucked in air, realizing my heart had picked up an extra patter. His charming smile was framed by his distinguished beard.

That face was familiar, beguiling. I returned the faint smile before deliberately looking away and moving along, not daring to give him a second glance.

We passed each other on aisle six. I didn't even make eye contact, instead I peered at the items before me, pretending I'd never seen so much foot lotion in my life. He cleverly bumped his cart against mine, muttered a deep, rumbled apology and moved a few feet away to look at the prophylactics.

And so we danced...

I grabbed a whisk to examine it.

He grabbed a glass jar of syrupy cherries.

I fondled a bag of walnuts.

He watched me through a jar of honey.

I licked my lips as I tried to decide which can of icing to get.

He made a big deal of sniffing a bottle of chocolate syrup.

Fine.

I stopped, pivoted the squeaky cart and moved on down to squeeze the Charmin.

He moved farther away to size up a large, black, phallic-looking flashlight. Then with a lecherous quirk to his lips, he grabbed some batteries.

Unreasonably annoyed and aroused, I turned away and this time I could've sworn I heard a chuckle as I left.

When I saw him a short distance from me at the deli section, I took my time viewing the large German sausages, the Portuguese linguisa and because I knew he was watching, I grabbed an exquisite ten-inch Italian salami.

Our eyes made contact and his gaze heated. This time he looked away. Feeling cocky, I smirked, dropped the salami into my basket and found myself following him as he stopped at the seafood counter where I watched him buy fresh oysters.

Oysters, my favorite sex food! Myth or not, those suckers could get my juices pumping!

I could hear him discussing cooking instructions with the clerk, the gentle baritone of his voice tugging at me whenever he spoke. I couldn't help but think of my husband and the way he liked to bury his face between my legs and go "oyster tasting," licking and pummeling me with his clever tongue until I was positively incoherent.

I stared blindly at a package of tofu, flushed, and felt a phantom sensual tug in my loins. Blinking several times, I finally realized I was still holding tofu. Tofu?

I put it back and moved away, feeling the man's gaze like a physical caress on my spine.

In the fruit-and-vegetable aisle he brushed past me as I contemplated lettuce, our clothes rustling softly as if apologizing to each other. I felt that brush of him, his clothes, the almost undetectable nudge of his semi-aroused penis, and the lingering effect of it almost made me weak.

In the reflective slant of a food guard, I peeked at him, admiring the way he held two small cantaloupes, roughly the same size as my breasts. Locking his gaze with mine, he lifted the fruit to his face and inhaled, bringing a sharp tightness to my nipples, causing them to strain. Those large, firm hands clutched the fruit with the power of a magician, linking the orbs to my breasts. Spellbound, I couldn't look away. Each time his thumb moved over the fruit, I felt it. Even the flicker of his tongue over his lips set my nipples more painfully against my shirt.

I waited, realizing I wanted to be where the fruit was, being touched by his hands and mouth, touched and licked by him, fondled by him....

He turned to add them to his shopping cart, and the spell was broken.

Like bumper cars, we turned and headed in opposite directions.

When he brushed past me again, I was standing by the plums and peaches. With a brief glance in his direction, I lifted the fruit and inhaled its ripeness. The plum looked especially succulent, firm and purple like the head of a stressed erection. I longed to nip the firm flesh, suck on it, taste the juices and feel them in my mouth, my throat.

Peaches are my husband's favorite. Once, long ago, drunk on wine and good soul music, I had halved a refrigerated peach and used it to stroke his length. I sandwiched his penis between the two halves and proceeded to stroke and suckle him simultaneously. Hot mouth, cold fruit. Despite the coolness, his erection had remained and I could see that the fibrous membrane was licking him almost as well as my tongue. I had tormented him for a long, long time, loving the helpless way he had begun to groan and thrust, ruining the fruit until it fell apart in my hands. I took the remains and stroked his testicles with it, then licked him clean.

When his fists had gripped the sheets in desperation, I whispered that I liked cream with my peaches and within seconds, he grunted and ejaculated in my mouth, chasing the sweet taste of the fruit with his own natural essence.

And yet here I was, my panties getting wet while I drowned in intimate memories.

"Need help with something?" a teenage clerk asked, interrupted my musing. I floundered before I blurted "No, thanks" in an embarrassingly husky voice.

I could also see that the man who'd been watching had strategically moved to stand behind his cart, but not before I saw his full arousal straining the front of his jeans. With an intense and promising gaze in my direction, he pushed his cart into another aisle.

I waited about ten seconds before I chased after him. By now my heart was beating wildly, my center had developed a deep pulse, and there was no hiding my extremely perky nipples.

I caught him at the cash register and felt a surge of disappointment. Was our game over so soon? Disheartened I moved to another open register and waited to be rung up.

I had just reached for my wallet when I glimpsed him again, finding a smile on his face. He winked discretely at me and I faked a brief wave as if he was my newspaper boy.

The distraction cost me, since now I had several items from our flirting that I certainly did not need. I was juggling the grocery bags in my arms when the whisk tipped over and fell out.

"Allow me." From behind me, the man's voice surrounded me like a scarf.

Feeling like a starstruck teenager, I could only watch as he retrieved it and placed it in my outstretched palm.

"Thanks," I said as my fingers curled around the handle. I suddenly realized he'd tucked a piece of paper in my hand along with the whisk.

"I'll see you around," he said and headed out of the door with his own grocery bag.

I managed to make it to the car before unfolding the note, which as it turns out was really his grocery receipt. In it there was the message: Three Palms Inn. Room 177.

I crumpled the note nervously in my fist, then after a few breaths, I opened it again and reread it.

Boy, he had nerve! Okay, so maybe I did stroke the thick salami in the deli and fondled the walnuts a bit intimately and...

Hunger for a different kind of salami and walnuts raged through me. I was really, really hungry.

I refused to second-guess myself as I started the car and left the parking lot, headed toward the inn. I was pulling into the parking lot when I saw him entering his room on the ground floor. He paused just slightly to look over his shoulder at me then went into his room.

I eased into a vacant spot, my hand sweaty on the stick shift. Taking a moment, I inhaled, exhaled, inhaled again. Finally, I decided that if I was going to do this, I had to do it right.

Reclining my seat slightly, I worked my panties over my hips, down my knees and off my ankles. They ended up in a wet heap under my seat, just like my bra. Nervously, I grabbed my purse and irrationally found myself stalling with the car door open. Should I or shouldn't I bring the salami to make a provocative opening remark? Hmmmm.

Nah. I settled for the peaches and threw a couple in my handbag. Then I locked the car, stopped by the nearby ice machine where I found an ice bucket still in wrapped in plastic. I filled it will ice, and went straight for Room 177.

After running a hand over my short braids, I knocked on the door. It opened to the gentleman wearing a white robe and an expression that was both mischievous and ardent. His eyes were the same shade of dark cocoa brown as his skin. His lips were full and tempting, his smile was pure seduction. For several seconds we let the heat simmer between us as we fully studied each other.

"Come in," he invited, his voice filled with a lover's promise and a spider's threat.

I stepped in and placed the bucket on the small table by the door, barely able to keep my eyes off him. The minute the door closed, I was pulled up against it, his body pressing sensually against mine, letting me know he was absolutely naked and hard beneath the robe.

I dropped my purse, and rocked instinctively against his hard-on, catching enough of a breath to meet his mouth-tangling kiss. And that's exactly what it was, our mouths tangling, tongues slipping and curling, tasting, sucking and devouring each other with almost immature finesse. God, I could hardly remember the last time I'd been kissed that way, and I've always loved a moustache, but his conservative beard was a wonderful extra sensation.

With a single move, his hands hungrily roamed over my breasts then my waist. With his tongue still plunging against mine, I wrapped my legs around his waist.

"Christ!" he blasphemed as his hands dropped to clutch my hips. He kissed me again, forcing a slower pace. The wide expanse of his hands slipped lower, moving to my thighs, then under my skirt and upward until his hands held my butt cheeks.

"Sweet," he murmured huskily when he realized I had forgone the underwear. He untied his robe, pulling it open and to the side. Already I could feel the head of his penis intimately introducing itself to me. Hello indeed!

We rocked together in mock thrusts, kissing and nipping our lips while our sexes lubricated on my dripping juices.

I wiggled once, impatiently, and ran my nails over his back. In a confident move, he adjusted his position and slipped into me in one long, hard, fluid motion. I cried out, part pain and the rest an incredulous riptide of pleasurable ripples.

"Ohhh...oh!" I clutched him, riding the spasms that came from being so thoroughly impaled by his shaft. He wasn't extremely thick, but he sure was long! I readjusted ever so slightly, for comfort, for pleasure. His harsh breathing was magnified in the silence. Against my chest, his fingers were busy undoing the buttons of my shirt until the garment hung open.

Then with his hot mouth sucking on my nipples he began to thrust into me, causing my body to thud slightly against the door. I moaned as the vaginal grip sent a sweet spiral up to my womb. Oh, God!

The rhythm was set, in and out, sex to sex, woman to man, until I hardly could think.

His teeth sank into my nipple in a soft bite, his groan trembling on my skin even as he whispered, "Yyyyesssss...."

I don't know if he was trying to hold back, but he suddenly seemed to lose the last of his control and he surged into me, hard, in brief, consecutive power thrusts that strained my thighs.

The final surge came like a roar, hard and overwhelming. His mouth slanted over mine, trembling as I felt his hot semen erupting deep within me.

I clutched him, feeling his legs lock and his buttocks clenching beneath my ankles.

It felt like forever that we stayed there, locked like mating insects, gasping for breath like asthmatic marathoners.

After a while, he seemed to regain strength and without separating, he carried me to the bed where we kissed leisurely for what felt like an endless moment.

He shrugged off his robe then rolled over so I could take off my shirt, then ever so gently, he withdrew his semi-aroused shaft from within me, allowing me to remove my skirt.

Seeing the reflection of the ice bucket in the mirror, I said, "Just a minute," and scrambled off the bed.

I figured he'd earned a free hind shot, so I bent over to dig in my purse for the peaches, then dunked them into the ice bucket, which I placed next to the bed. As I crawled back in, I noticed the bottle of chocolate syrup was on the night table, and the grin on his face was enough to make me chuckle. I guess he'd bought everything he put in his cart as well.

I loved it, being over him and seeing the natural turtleshell shape of the muscles of his abs. He reached for the chocolate syrup and rubbed two perfect rings into my nipples with his fingertips.

Keeping my eyes on his, I reached down and cupped his testicles, feeling the wetness of our release and massaging it into his bulbous weights and hardening cock. Then I moved the peak of my left breast over his waiting mouth, groaning when his teeth nipped my nipple and his lips assuaged the pain in multiple small sucks.

The smell of sex and chocolate filled the air with a sinful decadence, working on my system like fresh-baked pastry at a bakery.

I didn't realize my fist had tightened over his shaft until I heard, "Easy there" and felt his hand cover mine. Together, he sucked my sensitive breast while one hand covered mine over his penis, showing me the rhythm of strokes that he preferred. His other hand found my inner thigh, where my legs straddled one of his.

"Touch me," I whispered even as his fingertips traced my inner thigh, playing with my soft pubic hair. "Inside."

His touch was absolute torment, his fingers slipping between my labia, over my clitoris, stroking and rubbing with minimal penetration. It wasn't until I was jamming my hips against his hand that he began to plunge his thick fingers in, the slick, wet noise of it mixing with my moans when he simultaneously rubbed the heel of his palm on my sensitive clit.

By now my poor nipple was incredibly sensitive, but before I could say anything, he released it and latched on to the other one, giving it equal treatment.

My own pleasure was rolling in so hard and fast that I released his penis, braced my hands on his abs and rocked hard against his hand until I felt like I was melting over him. My voice released a garbled surrendering sound when I finally came, too weak to do anything but slump over him.

Breathing hard, he rolled me over onto my back a bit overeagerly. I didn't care. I was feeling drowsy and very satiated. I lifted my tired eyelids and found him licking the tip of his fingers, which had given me so much joy, the fires of desire burning hot in his eyes.

"Mmmm, you taste like wine-cooked oysters."

I smiled weakly and closed my eyes, but I could feel the bed shifting as he moved about. In truth, I wasn't expecting to feel his hands spread my thighs, nor to feel his mouth French-kissing my finger-romped vagina.

"Oohh," I complained weakly, "it's so sensitive. Please"

"I'm getting mine," he growled and continued the oral plundering as if I had hidden a treasure that he intended to recover with his tongue. His beard was wonderfully stimulating soft, ticklish, erotic. It wasn't long after that I was no longer complaining, but instead I was gripping the bed sheet in one hand and his head in the other.

Every lick and suck was so sensitive...so utterly sensitive....

"Pleeeease," I whispered.

"Yes," he agreed, and with a panther-like move he was over me, thrusting slow and long until he was sheathed completely inside me.

"Oh my," I whimpered in shameless delight.

His reply was a low, carnal grunt as me moved again, and again and again... Over and over, becoming harder thrusts, until the bed rocked, my breasts jiggled and I felt his rough ejaculation ripping through him. He fell on me, clutching me hard as the remaining shudder overcame him.

With his remaining strength, he cupped my buttocks and rolled over so as not to crush me. Minutes slipped by where all we did was catch our breath and listen to it until it became more even.

Entwined, with our flesh perspiring and semisticky, we rested and fell asleep.

I don't know why I awoke with a start, but I noticed that the alarm clock on the side table said I'd slept for about half an hour. The man was snoring softly, so I went to the bathroom and took a quick shower. It felt positively indecent to dress without my underwear, but I was really liking it.

As I stepped back into the room, I saw him propped on his side, waiting for me.

"You're leaving?" he asked.

"Yes, I have to go."

He just watched, his eyes eloquent.

"But there is one thing I forgot to do," I said and stepped back into the bathroom. I soaked a hand towel in warm water and took it with me to the bedside, to where his penis was once again tenting up the sheets.

"Lay back and enjoy," I said as I threw back the sheets to wash his phallus. When that was done, I reached into the ice bucket for a peach and used a plastic knife to cut it in half, removing the pit.

"What are you doing?" he asked gruffly.

"Having some peaches and cream," I replied saucily, giving him a wink.

"Are you keeping your clothes on?"

"Yup."

He grinned devilishly and settled more comfortably on the bed, parting his thighs for our mutual convenience. He even padded some pillows behind his back and head for a better view.

I grabbed the two juicy halves, positioned myself between his legs and touched them to the base of his cock.

His sharp hiss cut the silence as he tried to shrink away from the cold but his hips and cock remained thrusting outward. He withstood the way I rubbed the syrupy halves up and down his length, over the ridges of his eager stalk, circling the tip of his penis then down to the base, letting the fibrous membranes brush against his testicles. Indeed his erection went down, but not entirely.

"Cup the fruit in your hands," he commanded weakly and I did, making a virtual peach vagina where he thrust again and again. Soon the power of his thrusts smashed the fruit and all that was left was my wet hands on his penis, but I was already moving my mouth to catch the dribbling syrup. It was delicious, tasting the warmth of his skin and the coolness of the fruit.

I licked and nipped, cleaning up the fruit and gobbling noisily. My thumb followed my plundering mouth. Cresting the ridge of his ejaculatory path, I saw the sinews of his thighs tighten and strain with need.

"The peach was delicious," I murmured, using his penis like a microphone. "May I have some cream with it?"

"Yesss." He grasped my head and thrust into my mouth with a surrendering groan, filling the back of my throat with hot semen. I swallowed it greedily, licking whatever dripped over my lips and trailed on my chin. I held him there, in my warm oral kiss until the pulse of his penis became faint and soft.

I straightened, trying to ignore the orange stain in the front of my pristine white shirt and the heavy moisture between my thighs.

He looked so content, so defeated, so satisfied.

I bent over and kissed him. "Good-bye."

He reached for me. "Wait"

"I have to go," I said. He watched me for a minute before nodding.

I blew him a kiss and left, feeling wanton, crazy and as much a sensual woman as I'd felt in quite some time.

When I finally pulled up to my driveway, I was feeling warm from the memory. I sat behind the steering wheel, reliving the great details before finally prompting myself to throw my underwear into my purse, grab my groceries and head for the front door.

My keys hadn't even touched the door when the man's car parked behind mine and he stepped out, also grabbing his groceries. For an instant, our gazes connected and we shared a slow smile of lovers, of friends.

"There was an extra peach left," he said, the tone of his voice making me shamelessly aware of my lack of undergarments.

"Mmm, lucky you," I replied.

"Yeah. I kinda enjoyed the torture." His long stride brought him to me, but I focused on unlocking the door.

I stepped inside, with him half a step behind me. By his breath upon my neck, I could tell he'd been about to nibble on my ear when

"SURPRISE!" Several people shouted at once. "HAPPY ANNIVERSARY!"

I was so stunned I almost dropped the groceries.

"Mom! Dad!" my daughter exclaimed as she walked toward us. Christ! Everyone was there - neighbors, friends!

"Dad, you were supposed to keep her away for only half an hour. Where were you guys? You're late! "

"Stuff happens," he said with a noncommittal shrug. I turned toward my husband to yank on his skewered necktie. Oh, I could've strangled him!

My ever-inquisitive daughter looked into my husband's grocery bag. "A flashlight? Cherries ..."

"Well," I interrupted, "if I'm going to mingle, I should at least refresh myself."

My daughter placed the bag on the counter and reached for mine, leaving me no choice but to surrender it to her insistent hands.

"Mom, are you not wearing a bra?" My daughter gasped indelicately, her whispered mortification turning into a blush on her cheeks. Oh, great! I wondered who else had overheard.

"The strap broke," I lied lamely.

My husband came to the rescue by taking my hand and leading me away while instructing my daughter. "Sweetie, would you entertain while your mother and I go upstairs to change. We'll be down shortly."

We practically raced up the stairs, reluctantly falling back into our roles as parents and party hosts.

"Happy anniversary, love," he whispered, flashing me a smile that I never tired of seeing.

"Ditto," I replied, squeezing his hand. I was glad that I'd picked his favorite ice cream after all. And the peaches and...

I really have to go shopping more often!

Sand Surfing

Jackson absolutely amazes me. There are days when I can't believe I've hooked up with such an erratic, spontaneous, artistic soul. Quite unlike me in so many ways.

It had been almost a year since we first met at a friend's party. I'd determined he was not my type at all. And yet, before the night was over, I realized I was fascinated with him. Then as time went on, his charm wove a spell of magic around my heart. He's so unexpected, so uninhibited and fresh.

He was as much an American Indian as I was an African-American. Somewhere along the lines, we could only claim a quarter of true blood, but knowing that we had that in common made it special. He calls it "mixed mud" instead of "mixed blood."

My conservative ways drive him crazy, and his liberal ways often get on my nerves, but I'm learning to compromise.

And that was exactly why I'd agreed to travel with him for the next two weeks, driving crooked miles to an unknown destination. I had never taken a vacation without planning every minuscule detail, and when I first agreed to do this, I'd actually had to pop an antacid to keep my gut from roiling.

But at this point in our relationship, against my prissy nature, I agreed to do things his way, and I was somewhat surprised to find myself enjoying it.

Jackson's convertible car was his pride and joy. It looked like a seventies model, which I'm sure he'd resurrected from a junkyard and labored over it to create a beautiful mechanical masterpiece.

His road warrior was huge, painted a flawless, livid red. Orange and yellow painted flames roared from the tires and licked the base of the hood. The seats were spacious and cozy. And it could go from zero to zoom in a lightning blink.

One negative point was that it guzzled gas like nobody's business. But it throbbed like a Harley, which was worth extra points all the way around.

Personally I loved the deep, throaty sounds. Even when idle, the loud race-car growl of the engine shook the seats like a quarter-fed footmassager. I couldn't tell you the make or model, the number of horses that powered it or anything other than it was a monster of a car with a great purr. And just like its owner, I'd come to love it.

We had headed out of San Diego that morning while the day was still cool. After a short stop at the beach, we were back on the road. At some point, I pushed my passenger seat back far enough to stretch my legs out and relax. It was like laying on a twin-sized bed.

As the miles went by, the blur of wind and dry landscape coaxed me to sleep, murmuring secrets in my ears and painting my dreams in sea-filtered light. I was lost in watered green and blue sparks of sunlight, where I was making love, in so many ways; legs, limbs and accepting lips rubbed and stroked each other, making me yearn restlessly. I opened my mouth but could neither taste the textures nor drink the coolness of my dream. Deep inside, my hunger smoldered, my thirst increased and my body craved...craved...craved...

Much, much later, I barely registered the far-off hum of the convertible top coming down. It was the blazing sun on my body that eventually woke me. That, and the fact that the car no longer throbbed.

I peered at the driver's side, finding my bare-chested boyfriend watching me while popping candy into his mouth, grinning wickedly at me. His grin made him look like a lecher presented with a golden opportunity.

My eyes strayed to the candy in his hand and the smoldering intensified.

The man was addicted to sweets, and in my experience, almost never had sex without candy. Any evidence of them was as good as foreplay.

I became aware that my hands, which I had stretched above my head, had been handcuffed to the headrest. Jackson had taken the liberty of removing my bikini top, leaving my breasts to warm under the sun's furnace heat. Despite the sunblock, my nipples were already too hot in the exposure.

I wondered how I could've slept through the handcuffing process, but I'll admit I can sleep through almost any act of God. And besides, my dreams had been so very good.

"What's this?" I asked, tugging at the cuffs.

"Something new."

The gritty, unforgiving scorch was parching my throat clear through. Because of my reclined position, I had to crane my neck to see outside. All I saw was a vast flatness of desert that stretched all the way to the horizon. Above us a blazing cloudless sky domed as blue as an inverted ocean. Jackson seemed right at ease in the middle of it all, like part of the landscape.

"Wh-where are we?" I asked.

"The desert. I grew up around here. I know it like the back of my hand." He popped another chewy candy into his mouth then offered me a sip from his sports bottle. "Here, have some. You look a bit thirsty."

The water was cold enough to give me a delicious tingle as it went down. I gulped it greedily until he pulled the bottle away. He dribbled a few freezing droplets on my exposed nipples, eliciting an unexpected groan from me.

Jackson chuckled with devilish merriment as my breathing increased. He moved over to my side, kneeling at my feet, then leaned over my body, beginning to lick my belly button as if it was my kiss-starved mouth.

The lick and suckle of my belly button fed the fire in me, causing me to suck in my abs.

My voice was a squeak as I arched my back. "Ahhh, Jackson!"

"Hmm?" The sound vibrated against my skin, sizzling there. Already he was busy unzipping my shorts, then slipping his hands beneath the jeans and fondling my hip bones, my thighs, the crest of my pubic hair where my mois-

64

ture was starting to seep. Every touch undid a part of my clothing, denuding me until I wore nothing but handcuffs. And although my thighs were now spread, my sex exposed, I was still denied the slightest penetration.

He took a momentary break to sip cold water, to watch me pant, to eye my wetness. Then lowering his head again, he blew once on my clitoris before boisterously nuzzling it, slipping his cold tongue into the moist folds of my vagina, spreading my thighs wider to greedily access my trove.

Behind my tightly shut eyes, colors formed at the oral brushstrokes. Orange and coral red began to blend with each lick, succumbing to each other with each wicked swipe of his talented tongue. In my mind's eye, pink crested pale yellow, burning hot like my lips and nipples. Still he went on as if unquenched by all my wetness, which flooded his lips. He consumed me like a lion on a meal, licking and nuzzling and nipping all parts of my vagina until I could hardly breathe.

He hummed on my clitoris, blowing on my hot skin, sipping the cold water to make a contrast of his mouth, causing me to shiver again. Behind my eyelids, a wide ocean of colors infused my mental sky, threatening to drown me in its pleasure.

Far sooner than I had expected, the soundless thunder of his tongue unleashed a climax that hit me so strongly, my eyes fluttered. My body pulsed thickly, and I was unable to even utter a moan. The ocean of colors poured over me, airless, weightless and hard enough to shudder the breath from my lungs.

My hands were helpless as they tugged on the cuffs, my breath faltered and my existence was completely at the mercy of his mouth. "Oh, ohhh!"

Time suspended and endless moments later, I felt Jackson move, leaving me weak-limbed and spent.

When I heard him again, he was naked, positioning my legs around his hips, placing my feet on the large dashboard. His large, erect penis rubbed over my clitoris with uncertain restraint, then the luscious friction of his eager tip slipping over my folds.

How beautiful he was, leaning over me with such dominance, the muscles of his arms and chest bunched and stressed with tight control, his skin as brown as the desert I'd seen, his shoulder-length hair falling over onto my face.

"I can never get enough of you," he said in genuine bewilderment, as if my reply would be something I myself could comprehend.

"Oh, Jackson," I whispered, completely humbled.

Inch by precious inch, the thickness of him moved into me, stretching until his entire length was snug inside me. The brush of his body against mine turned into a full-body contact. The fine hairs on his legs caressed my inner thighs, our pelvises were locked in the most primal of flesh sockets as his chest hairs rubbed my abraded nipples and the candy-cunt smell of his breath brushed against my mouth.

"Goddamn beautiful," he swore huskily as he thrust in one slow, initiating caress. His eyes were hazel, but the blue in them was as true as the sky above us. His breath shivered with careful control. "I've been dreaming of this."

I kissed him in amazement as my body began to tingle again. His mouth tasted of my sex, watermelon candy, sunblock and sweat, blending together into a fiercely arousing flavor. The slickness of our sweat added to the ravaging of my senses.

Then as if he'd forgotten something, he stopped, gasping for air and control. In my vaginal passage, I could feel his cock pulsating, twitching ever so slightly.

"I want to take you on a ride," he said, withdrawing his length slightly from within me.

Lightheaded with passion, I nodded.

He grinned and reached over to the ignition to start the car. The speakers came to life, blasting loudly with the solo drum recording he'd been working on for his band. The sounds of it competed with the rumble of the engine. Jackson prodded an odd-looking hiking stick between the gas pedal and the driver's seat.

The car lurched forward like an unleashed beast and the blistering desert wind fanned over us. Adrenaline seared a screaming path to my brain.

"Oh, God! What are you doing? Are you crazy?" I tugged helplessly at the handcuffs.

"Trust me," he whispered in my ear. "Trust me!"

He silenced me with the force of his kisses, working a steady rhythm of sexual thrust and punts that plowed deep into me.

I could hear the gravel churn beneath the tires as the car tore down the open desert. The panic brew in my veins was now mixing with the uncomfortable, intense pleasure delivered in each thrust that poked deep in my womb, knocking upon that elusive G-spot.

I moaned and struggled, wavering between a horrible fear of dying this way and the need to match his thrusts to get my sacred orgasm. I could feel it rising quicker than it ever had, and I found myself wishing my hands were free to touch myself.

Several thrusts later, he grit his teeth and withdrew completely. "Turn over!"

"Jackson"

"Now!" His penis glistened wetly and I hurried to do as he said, noticing he'd left just enough slack in the handcuffs for my wrists to shift around and still be comfortable. I could feel the shock absorbers of the car adjust to the ribbed terrain, jostling us slightly.

My alarm hiked at my new view of the landscape. At least when I was laying down, I felt safer.

Now, I wanted to scream with fright. The overwhelming sound and force of the wind pushed against me, the rumble of the car was accentuated by occasional jostling, and worse of all, I could now see just how fast we were barreling across the desert while we romped.

I helplessly watched the dust trail behind us in shock, trying to calm my frightened heart when he mounted my vagina from behind with renewed vigor.

"Aaaahh!

My cry was snatched by the wind and demolished by the deafening music. My lover rode me like a stallion dominating a mare, the force of it jostling my breasts and almost shoving me face down into the seat. Either fear or desire or the mere need to sustain my position worked to tighten my muscles, making my passage a tighter, wetter grip, making me tremble with pleasure.

His partial words reached me. "Oh, honey. Aahh...yes..."

Again and again, he ground in and out of me, harder, faster and faster, until I felt like the speed of the car, the force of the thrust and the seduction of the desert set us in another unique dimension that defied definition.

The only laws of physics that applied were the mechanics of wetness, piston plunges and crotch-clenching quivers.

Jackson's sex invaded me until I knew he was about to come undone. Each thrust was too much, yet not quite enough. The wind now had the touch of a voyeur lover. The heat of the desert cupped us everywhere. I'd never felt so heated, frightened and alive!

With a cry of wild abandon, Jackson ejaculated, spewing his hot semen into the depths of my womb. My inner thighs strained to hold him, my body wanting to suckle him deeper still, wishing he wouldn't stop. Unable to help it, I kept rocking against him, riding out my own quicksilver need, angling to my G-spot.

I pushed backward hard into his cock, and like a bull's-eye, his penis met its mark, sending my thighs and womb quaking. I became pure woman, turned to water, sun then sea-dreamed colors for each one of those liquid spasms. He was still hard enough to thrust until I couldn't take anymore.

Finally spent, I turned my head to see him, but all I got was my hair back on my face and the sun in my eyes.

Jackson bent over me, cupping and molding my breasts as he rocked his spent cock in the aftermath of my orgasm. Peripherally, I saw him reach for the hiking staff and give it a tug to remove it.

The car immediately began to slow, which was a good thing because the landscape was much more uneven now. I finally gave in and lay sandwiched between his hot body and the familiar shaking of the seat.

With his limp cock still in me, he reached for the small keys in the ashtray and unlocked the handcuffs as we rode more uneven terrain at a slower pace. Whenever the tires wobbled, we wobbled. Such sweet agony.

"So, whatcha think?" he asked weakly when he finally settled back into the driver's seat.

I sat back down with an exhausted sigh, smearing the musky wetness on the seat and running my hands over my wrists. I could hardly believe I'd just had a bit of bondage sex in a speeding car, in a desert of all places. "I think I'm going to like taking more vacations with you."

Virtual Bliss

They call us MUD heads. Nerds who like to play in Multiuser Domains. I belonged to an exclusive underground world of computer addicts who had become tired of the way society viewed us. I mean, so what if we could debate ad nauseum on binary strategies, digital benchmarks and the superior programming advantages of Linux? We were ambitious, maybe a bit kinky, but smart and inventive.

Smart enough to come together to program our own entertainment, our virtual world of holographic designs, consisting of westerns and futuristic games to comics to global myths. Not only did it keep us physically fit, but it sharpened our minds. And then us ladies got tired of mayhem and gore and put together a little game for ourselves. Some of the men helped, of course.

This was where I stood now, in the middle of Breath of Kilimanjaro, an African mythology adventure where the object of the game was something much more pleasurable.

I entered the virtual parlor garbed in nothing but my electrosensitive African panga (Swahili for machete). My nipples and my clit had penny-sized vibrators. These remote-access gadgets, called burrs, had been sticky-taped on to hold them in place. They were activated upon some whim by an unknown sequence, and could become a seriously delicious distraction.

Sometimes they made me so completely aroused that I was very tempted to just abandon the game and find my own jolting orgasm. And to be completely honest, that might be why I never made it past level two of this game.

But right now, the suckers were warm, but unmoving. And I really, really wanted to win this level.

I adjusted the gel-soft phallic grip that served as a handle to my panga and squinted into the darkened cavern through the 3-D eye contacts.

From the left a virtual bat flew at me, and I swung my weapon, slicing it and making it disappear in a puff of smoke. I could hear a beast moving around in the shadows of the virtual jungle, making the stealthy noises only a large predatory creature can make. I could feel the misty chill of Nenaunir, the Masai demon, a spirit of evil.

A rattler warned off at a distance, sending a shiver up my spine, telling me I was closer to my goal than ever before. I moved cautiously, feeling a breeze to my left and sensing my back was too exposed. Instead, I realized what appeared to be the breezelike movement of leaves on the trees were actually forms of virtual beings, morphing out of the woodwork and surrounding me. The moan of the wind became the moan of lovers as tree limbs became parted arms, legs and mouths.

The illusion shimmered, the surrounding forest becoming groups of naked humans, groups intensely involved in joining hips and tongues and invasive grips that looked like a wallpaper of orgies come to life. Bodies were sandwiched, some restrained, others bent for any service of sex.

I stood frozen, equally fascinated and unnerved by their carnal boldness and yet feeling my wetness suddenly seeping between my thighs. I should have guessed it was a diversionary tactic, because no sooner had I stopped to watch them than I felt the whiplash sting on my buttocks. I whirled around, panga raised, and encountered the beast awaiting.

Finally!

It was a lavish, enormous creature with the dark-gold pelt of a lion, but the black face of a crude villainous mask. When we'd programmed this, we'd argued among ourselves too much to settle on a mythical god, so we'd ended up making a fictitious one. And now, even as adrenaline surged to bond with fright, I admired that face.

"So, you are the one they send after me! You think you can defeat me!" he bellowed, his tremendous penis twitched, aroused and erect in velvet brown between his legs. Even knowing that it was all a clever illusion, I swallowed in newfound fear and excitement.

Its tail lashed out, almost catching me again. I swung my panga, but my movements were too slow, too late.

He prowled closer. "You're going to bend for me. You will submit to me and I will have you like"

"Never!" I vowed, pointing my panga.

We circled each other, him snarling and growling, one paw raised as if to swipe the life from me. I could hear him breathing, smell the sweat of something male and wild. Unexpectedly, the tiny burrs came to life against my skin, creating an erogenous triangle that sent a hot flash of tingles over my body.

"Ahhh," I gasped involuntarily at the delicious sensation, trying to refocus on the proximity of the beast. My knees trembled and in my hand, the phallic gel like grip of the panga felt remarkably real.

"Surrender," he whispered throatily, "and I will be merciful."

"I will defeat you!" I swore, as I lunged at him, plunging my panga into the roll of his feline shoulder.

He roared in anger, and for a flash of a second, his image changed, revealing the African prince warrior trapped in the hideous spell, then the wound healed in a bright show of light, and he became the beast again.

Snarling angrily, he retaliated, his paw smacking painlessly against me, yet hard enough to send me tumbling on the ground. I was quick to recover, however, and rose in a crouch.

Around me the naked bodies were mating, rutting and groaning in escalating tones. I could see the mechanics of it, the pistonlike rutting, jaws and throats working in suction of flesh, their uncontrolled ecstatic expressions. I suddenly wanted to be one of them, to be fiercely surrounded.

The beast leaped toward me and I quickly tumbled again, managing to use my panga as I rolled to slash his underbelly.

Once again, the injury brought a savage roar, but I saw my handsome African prince again and while the image was still flickering, I hurled my panga at the beast, hearing its computer-generated gurgle of complete defeat.

There was a moment of total darkness then a sudden storm brewed out of nowhere, filling my vision with several flashes of lightning and the deafening rumble of thunder. With the tempest breaking above me, my body burrs began to hum so hard that I staggered and fell weakly to the ground, slipping my desperate fingers to where the mind-shattering orgasm was quickly overtaking me.

Through my half-open eyelids, I saw the spotlight of where the beast had been and where now my large African prince had metamorphosed, curled in the same position in which I'd vanquished the creature. The spotlight dimmed until I was left alone with him in the pitch darkness.

Yet, I couldn't even react when I heard him approach me, felt his presence near me, positioning over me. "You came," his whisper, dark and excited. Sounding like freedom.

I vaguely wondered whether he was referring to the rescue or my lack of control. I'd never programmed the game this far.

Without expecting a response, he clasped my hands above my head. The light was still too saturated with shadows for me to see him clearly, but I could make out his brawny physique, the hungry, lusting gleam in his eyes. I could smell the scent of his eager sex.

"You freed me," I said as he spread my thighs. "You saved me!"

I smiled weakly, still feeling somewhat incoherent from the tiny vibrators.

"Is this your mighty weapon?"

He held the phallic grip of my panga, which he had retrieved. The blade had been removed and he was now using the soft dildo end to nudge urgently between my thighs.

"Warrior princess," he whispered, pushing the first half inch in, then thrust deeply until I was forced to squirm to accommodate it, gasping and arching in a mixture of excitement, pleasure and pain.

My groan echoed in the cavern as if I was dying, each plunge of the panga was almost more than I could bare. The small burrs were back in buzzing action, and I could hear the slippery wetness as my slit sucked greedily on the long gel-like grip of the panga.

"You broke the spell," he said, breathing huskily, his mouth sucking on the exposed parts of my breasts, my belly. I could feel the contours of his hard thighs beside mine, his hot breath against mine, his hardened lengthy penis and weighed testicles rubbing against my thigh, imitating the rhythm of the panga.

"Oooohh, yes...please...ahhhh...yes, yes...pleaseeee!" I begged.

But his knuckle brushed against my labia, his thumb flicking over my clit again as the panga grip impaled me again. On and on it went, my vagina becoming more sensitive and raw with greed, my voice hoarse from panting, my shameless whimpers echoing into spirals in the cavern.

He released one of my hands and prepared to mount me when I noticed that the darkness above me was beginning to acquire a glow.

"Put me in," he ordered.

I reached for his rigid shaft, giving a quick squeeze and stroke before placing his impressive cock at my wet portal. I waited, moving my hand to briefly stroke his testicles then move them to the firm muscles that clenched his buttocks.

With an uninhibited grunt he thrust in completely. Crying out as his thickness, which docked hard into me, I farther widened my thighs. His breathy words became sacred murmurs on my skin, wrapped in the mystical cadence of a chant, shaky from the thrusts of his arousal. Not only did his hard body grind the shivering burrs farther against me, but the added friction of his hard, muscled skin kept me tossing on a peak that threatened to undo my control.

Each plow rippled into my passage, each withdrawal made me yearn for more, and much sooner than I had expected, I found myself screaming out my second climax, clutching him as if I would drown.

And indeed I did feel as if I was drowning, floating away into a funnel of emotion that stemmed from the depths of my vagina. Finally, I lay replete and reeling, my body still absorbing his continuous rough plunges. I could tell he was close to losing control by the intensified clutch of his hands and the urgency of his breathing. His clever mouth licked the taste from my neck, searched for my pulse to suckle it.

As his tempo increased, he sank his teeth gently into my earlobe, commanding, "Turn and suck it."

I opened my eyes to peer into the dim light, finding the moistened panga grip now laying inches from my lips, held there by his fisted hand even as he kept rocking more firmly into me. In the jewel light, the fake penis glistened from being inside me earlier.

I flicked my tongue at the pseudo-phallus, tasting myself there before placing pouty kisses on the fleshlike tip of the dildo. I used my tongue to flick it, swirl around it, stroking and nipping the length like a delectable ice cream cone.

"More! Suck more!" He grunted and I could feel his penis thickening inside me, arousing me all over again as his tempo increased. So I turned my head more fully and suckled the flesh-like grip of the panga until it filled my mouth.

"Yes! Yes!" He groaned, jolting my body with his strength. His thumb must have flicked a hidden switch because suddenly I could taste a sweetness seeping from the plum tip of the dildo. I sucked harder, deeper, noisily drawing out this delicious honey taste and feeling like I was sucking and fornicating him at the same time.

My womb began to shiver with pleasurable aftershocks when he suddenly lunged hard, grinding into me and moaning as he sank a viciously sensual love bite at the pulse on my throat, his thighs pinning me, his torso dominating me as he delivered the ultimate plunge.

I felt his hot release squirting into my depths, and my jaw quivered as I sucked harder on the dildo wishing it was his hot fluid flooding my mouth.

Finally he relaxed upon me, growing heavy, his ribs shifting with each raspy breath. I pushed the sword grip from my mouth and turned my head toward his, taking his tongue avariciously while my vaginal muscles tightened experimentally around him.

The burrs still hummed in a low key, intensified by the trapped slickness of our perspiring bodies. He exacerbated the process by moving over me to share the torment, moving slowly...slowly over me.

Minutes later, in a quick move, he rolled our bodies until I lay over his. I slipped his penis out of me, then removed the sticky tape that had kept the tiny burr against my sensitive nub. I carefully placed it at the base of his limp cock, right where the testicles met the neck of his penis, like a gift.

He acquiesced with a quiet moan, murmuring something dark and erotic that twirled inside my skin like sunlight. Then because I enjoyed his second moan, I wrapped my lips around his semi-aroused erection and leisurely sucked it.

Ah, this was definitely not a sword grip, and I had no doubt that when he was completely hard, it would be a difficult organ to accommodate in my mouth. But for now, I played with him, licking and stroking, feeling the tiny tremors of the burr until the renewed strength flowed back into his penis, making it plump meat in my mouth.

With a final lick, I wiggled over his black, muscular body to straddle his handsome face. I watched him for a few seconds, admiring the angles of his jaw, the full lips, the distinctive wide nose. Oh, he was handsome all right! Giving him no option, I shifted over him until my nether lips were over his mouth. My knees tightened over his ears and I cupped his tight haircut to hold him in place, selfishly looking for my own pleasure now. Let him breathe through his ears, I thought wickedly.

His large hands palmed my buttocks and his mouth slanted over my pubis, his tongue exploring my sensitive skin only to punish it with gentle nips of his teeth.

The ride was slow and easy, growing as he lengthened the torment. It wasn't much longer before I was moaning and gyrating on his face. I moved my hands to cup my breasts, feeling the heat of the buzzing burrs on my tender skin. I tried to be considerate of him but his tongue was making me wild, stroking, curling and sucking on my folds and nub until I couldn't stand it anymore.

I needed him! I needed to feel his length and breadth in me, battering those delicious strokes into me. I jumped off his face and knelt within arm's reach.

"Now!" I said urgently, my voice hitching. "Now!"

He was on me like a dog before I could finish my request, his straining cock slipping into my lubricated passage with renewed vigor. His hands were clamps on my hips, uncompromising as he plowed again and again into my eager soreness.

When he curled over me and cupped my vibrating nipples, I barely cried out when I felt my muscles convulse around him like sea-quaked water. My open mouth sucked in musky air, yet all my breath felt snatched from my lungs. I felt my very bones ripple until my eyes closed and my body coasted on air...suspended.

His deep, triumphant shout sounded as if from a distance yet my body still registered the rush of semen bathing my cervix, the friction of his hips gliding against my buttocks, the ramrod firmness of being completely and thoroughly mounted without moving.

Endless moments later, he turned me on my back, kissing me on the lips, this tongue familiar, the intimate taste of our mutual sex flavoring his kiss. I felt too weak to even kiss him back with conviction, but at last my brain, my skin and even the burrs had stopped humming.

I must have dozed because when I awakened again, I was alone, sexually exhausted. Overhead the lights flickered on and I lay in the empty holographic suite, listening to the computer offer me congratulations as it politely informed me I had passed on to level three.

Yes, I thought with a satisfied smile, only seven more levels to go and I'll have this game beat.

Deadlines

I was hired to do a job of three people by myself. Mainly because I'm damned good at what I do, and secondly because I'm neurotic when it comes to deadlines. 'The powers that be had' set up my computer den in the new wing of Orion Securities, on a special assignment for "a very important client". I knew immediately I'd be living on caffeine and donuts for the next month for this "special" client.

The pay almost made up for the intense, maddening long hours where all the UNIX, Linux and SQL commands were starting to run together. And did I forget to mention that we were having air conditioning problems? I swear, the room was cool probably one hour of each day. For the rest of the time, I perspired and prayed like crazy that the computers wouldn't suddenly fizzle in a hot puddle of circuitry.

So I was in no mood to crack a smile when my boss came in to check on me before the deadline, just one of his annoying habits.

So just to irk him, I kept my answers vague, still typing on my computer as I did so. Truth be told, I was ahead of schedule, but he didn't need to know that yet.

"Hi, Keisha. We thought you might need some help," he said in his car salesman voice, "So we hired Mr. Jacob Wong to help out with Phase Three."

Now, let me explain. I'd just worked fifteen hours, and had no time for this interruption, much less the added factor of acquiring someone new to mess up my work. I whirled my chair around ready to do battle. "Excuse me?"

Immediately I noticed the frown on my supervisor's face when he saw I had changed my business suit to shorts and a T-shirt. I raised my eyebrow, silently daring him to say something. I mean they weren't spandex tight or even indecent. And besides, this was my third day of complaining about the heated conditions. Hey, if he wanted the machines to blow up, cool, but I was not going to roast all day in a suit.

Reluctantly he sighed. "May I introduce to you, Mr. Jacob Wong."

The man next to my boss smiled and politely extended his hand. "Please call me Jake."

Some lame part of my mind was aware that I'd stopped chewing my gum to look at this man from head to toe. Okay, so he wasn't just Asian, but African-Asian. He wasn't exactly tall, but he looked like he was built lean and stocky. His tight military haircut and intelligent gaze met mine and then I saw his dimple. Ahhh, dimples. They get to me every single time.

Although he wasn't GQ handsome, he did have the look of quiet patience, which was offset by the look of mischief in his eyes. I raised an eyebrow in silent inquiry, wondering what the hell he found amusing. He raised his, and I noticed a ghost of a smile played on the corner of his mouth.

My boss cleared his throat, and I realized I'd left them hanging. Trying to act as professional as my clothes and mind allowed, I reached for Jake's outstretched hand and shook it, saying "Pleasure to meet you. I'm Keisha."

Mmm, long fingers. Nice grip. What else you got?

"Pleasure's all mine.," he replied in a smooth, polished voice that still managed to bring to mind rumpled sheets and sweat-gasped promises.

I tried to mentally shake off the evocative thought. Too much caffeine, candy and endless working hours, I reasoned. It had to be what was firing up my hormones.

I pretended to listen while my boss rambled about the project and Jake's new role.

"The nightly batch processes to track the resources."

Yeah, I did that already. I tried to hold back an exasperated sigh, but Jake must have noticed. Either that or he was temporarily fascinated with my breasts.

"Client submissions from the web to integrate with the accountable items."

Yeah, I'd finished that too.

Jake was nodding occasionally, yet I saw his gaze turn ever so briefly to my ankles, my bare legs, my cleavage and finally my face. Between one blink and the next, the sensual intensity of his gaze seared me. I was stunned that he would be so bold.

Both in tech school and at my nerdy job, I'd dealt with men of all kinds. But I'd never felt such a strong sexual attraction to an Amerasian before.

My boss was wrapping up whatever he was saying, ending with, "and I hope you enjoy working with us, Jake."

"Most definitely," Jake said, looking cool and professional again. I don't think my boss even noticed the sparks flying between us.

"Okay. I'll leave you two together and I'll come back in a while to check on things."

As he headed out the door, I could already see a sheen of sweat on my boss' brow.

"Mac," I called before he could make his exit. "Could you please have maintenance do something about this heat? The computers can't take much more of it."

"Absolutely. They promised to fix it today," he said and left. It was the same answer he'd given me before.

Jake removed his jacket, loosened his tie and sat at one of the empty terminals. "So, what do you want me to do?"

The sexual possibilities made my mind go blank for a full second. To compensate, I took some much-needed time to grab paperwork from my desk then went over to where he sat. I handed him a stack of diagrams and notes and began to explain the next part of the project in need of development.

This much I was serious about, so I didn't so much as bat my lashes at him.

No point messing up all my hard work just because I found the man sexy as hell.

I sat on the edge of his desk and crossed my legs as if I was wearing a business suit, feeling quite a bit underdressed. He asked intelligent questions and seemed knowledgeable enough about the intricacies of the project.

When I leaned forward to point out something on the paperwork he was reading, his gaze left the paper and traveled to where my cleavage was proudly displayed. He took a good, long, appreciative look then went back to the page.

Oh yeah. He was definitely interested. Heck, my nipples were hard as diamonds about it.

Muttering his thanks, he began to gather the documents.

"Ah, well, if you have any questions, don't hesitate to ask," I said and returned to my computer.

It wasn't long before I heard his rapid-fire fingers dancing over the keyboard. Good. That in itself spoke volumes about his computer skills.

I refocused my attention to where I'd left off in my programming and deliberately lost myself in my world of codes.

As it happens when I concentrate on my work, time flew by to the background sonata of typing and to my internal realm of logic and procedures. And it wasn't until my watch alarm went off, informing me I'd worked sixteen hours straight, that I finally took a break.

I turned to see Jake deeply engrossed in his work. The heat was smothering and I wanted nothing more than to fan my tanktop. Jake had a light sheen of sweat, but looked relatively cool.

"How's it going?" I asked.

"Good," he said, his fingers typing slower as he wrapped up a segment of code. "I think I'll have most of this finished by tomorrow."

"That'd be excellent," I said as I turned off my computer. "Come on, shutdown. It's time to go."

He nodded and began to do so. I straightened in my chair, trying to relieve the kinks from my spine. I closed my eyes and turned my neck, easing the tightness in my shoulders.

I heard his computer power down, but I jerked when I felt his warm hands touching my shoulders.

"It's just me," he reassured, removing his hands. I couldn't see him to read his expression, and I certainly hadn't heard his silent stride when he moved behind my chair.

"Okay," I replied. His strong fingers brushed past my short braids to return to my shoulders, squeezing the tension right out of my tired muscles. I moaned with a pleasure that sounded sexual but was not even remotely associated. "That feels so wonderful."

"Had a long day?"

"Mmmm," I mumbled, wanting the sensations to never end. "Long day. Sixteen hours."

The massage went on for a few more minutes until I was aware of those fingers in an entirely new way. I could smell the light, masculine scent of his cologne and the heat in the room was making my skin overly sensitive.

We heard the door down the hall open and close, then the overweight footsteps of my boss as he approached.

I touched Jake's hands just before he removed their magical touch. "Thanks."

I tipped my head back to see him, but his expression was hooded. "You're welcome."

When our boss showed up at the door, I had gathered my purse and keys and Jake had gathered his stuff.

I could feel my body shutting down, so I didn't linger with good-byes. I managed to make it to my hotel room where I simply fell on the bed and slept like a rock, dreaming of Jake's magic touch cresting over my entire body.

* * *

The following day, I dressed in a thigh-high denim skirt and a yellow button-down shirt. I would've bet anyone a hundred bucks that the cooling system was still not working.

And I was right. More than right. The place seemed to have gone up ten degrees more than yesterday.

I was standing there fuming when Jake stepped into the office, wearing navy slacks with his white shirt and blue tie. My boss had made an early appearance and placed two standing fans by the computers.

"Oh, I don't believe this," I said, noticing that the idiot had plugged the fans to the main computer power supply.

Jake looked diplomatic as he gave his response. "Hmm."

I went to my desk and picked up the phone to speed-dial my boss and give him an earful about the laws regarding working conditions and the unpleasant alternatives. He hemmed and hawed but promised to come up with a better solution.

I finally slammed the phone down and turned to see Jake smiling hugely. "What?" I growled.

He burst out laughing and my anger evaporated.

"Boy, you sure get on a roll when you're mad," he observed.

I shook my head, reluctantly smiling. "I have little patience with incompetence."

"Hey, we're all human," he said, playing devil's advocate.

"But not all equal."

His smile lingered and his voice dropped slightly, the depths of his eyes getting darker. "Thank God."

Now, why did I get the impression he was talking about the differences in our genders? I hid my smile by walking off to prepare a pot of coffee and soon we were back at work. When lunch came around, Jake agreed to pick up the Chinese food while I stayed at my desk.

I waited until ten minutes after he left then I couldn't stand it anymore. I went to one of the fans and stood in front of it, letting the delicious flow of cool,

cool air hit me. But it wasn't enough, so I undid my shirt and bra, and exposed myself to the breeze from the whirling blades.

"Ooooh, yeah," I groaned. I arched my neck and let the air hit me there, then my face and hair. It felt truly wonderful as it blew the gleam of sweat right off my skin.

I'm not sure what alerted me, but I glanced at the door to find Jake standing there, the food in his hands and his intense focus on my breasts.

I gasped and whipped my shirt closed.

"Don't stop on my account." Although he smiled, his voice was husky and his hardening penis was starting to tent his pants.

With an embarrassed chuckle, I turned from him and refastened my bra, my fingers fumbling with the larger buttons of my shirt.

"Where did you learn to walk like that, so quietly?" I asked, trying to change the subject.

His smile widened, but his gaze remained hot. "Ancient Chinese secret."

"Right."

I pushed my chair near his desk and ignored my perky nipples in favor of digging in the cartons of food. The bite I had set my mouth on fire.

"Hot damn," I gasped, reaching for the soda he handed me. "What was that?"

"Szechuan Chicken. Spicy food is supposed to cool your body's inner temperature. Here, I'd better give you this."

I sucked down soda, warily eyeing the Beef Broccoli.

"Thanks," I said and took an experimental bite. Not bad. We ate through the awkward silence, my gaze occasionally flittering to his groin where his semi-erect penis still nested and his eyes occasionally going to my breasts.

There was no hope of my breasts looking normal now!

To relieve the tension, I began talking about the project. Jake listened and commented, but our attention was definitely diverted.

Finally, I rose to put away the food in the break room down the hall. Jake walked past me to use the men's rest room.

I'd put everything in the fridge and had closed the door when I heard the crystal clear-rush of running water. With a frown I looked around, finally realizing that the sound seemed to come from the pantry.

It turned out that the noise emanated from a vent above a door and lucky for me, a ladder was positioned nearby. I quietly moved it next to the vent, climbed and peered through to find a surprising view of the men's room.

Jake was leaning over the sink, filling his hands with water and then washing his face. He looked at his reflection and shook his head.

"Damn breasts," I heard him clearly mutter, but there was no one there but him.

Using several paper towels, he dried his hands and face, then tossed the paper in the bin to glare at himself in the mirror. With a sigh, he nudged the bunk of his penis in his pants, as if to make it less noticeable.

First to the left. Then to the right, followed by a few small hops. It still looked like he was hiding a banana down his pants. Sighing heavily, he ran an exasperated hand over his hair then walked into a stall right under my sights.

The chuckle I'd been holding in vanished when he leaned against the door and unzipped his slacks. I watched greedily, envying his hands when he lowered the underwear, revealing his turgid brown erection.

He closed his eyes, leaned his head back and began to stroke himself. The gentle clink of the belt matched the rhythm of his hand and even from where I was I could hear his breath quickening. His beautiful penis thickened at the manipulation of each stroke, the plump tip hardening while I wished I could lick and swallow the length of aroused flesh.

Dry mouthed, I watched Jake's face grow taut, tension making him brace his shoulders against the door of the stall. The first creamy drop glistened on the head of his cock then two strokes later, he groaned through clenched teeth, his ejaculation squirting up from the pumping grip of his cock.

"Umhh!"

His strokes slowed and his head lowered tiredly to examine the mess. His legs must not have been steady since he leaned a hand against the wall and waited a few moments longer before cleaning himself.

My own legs were none too steady, my own arousal now up several notches. God, I was supposed to keep my mind on work after seeing this? All I would be thinking of was that his erection could have been put to better use. Like deep inside me.

I gripped the ledge of the vent, closed my eyes briefly and touched my now-wet vagina, rubbing in circles to ease the carnal need there. I heard the squeaky stall door and opened my eyes to see Jake buckling his belt.

He washed his hands with deliberate slowness, the water running over his wrists for a long while, but he avoided his reflection. When he headed for the door, I quietly stepped down from the ladder and raced back to my desk.

Back in my chair, I typed anything just to keep some sound in the room. I was so aware of him, from when he sat down to when he started typing again. His fingers were slow and sluggish and after a few seconds he hit a key that brought about a series of compilation error beeps.

Peripherally, I saw him glimpse at me then run a hand over his hair, exactly the same way as he had in the rest room.

I was hot from the inside out! And wet. And seriously bothered. The air was stifling, my code was crap and any moment now, I'd do something stupid like hit the wrong keys that would cause my computer to chirp as well.

I deleted my code to restart then realized we were both waiting, our fingers poised over our respective keyboards. The tension billowed like steam between us.

He didn't even turn my way when he said, "Nice nails."

I frowned at the odd comment, splayed my fingers and noticed the hot red nail polish I'd painted on the morning before. Shit!

"I barely caught a glimpse of the color from the sink."

I briefly closed my eyes and curled my fingers into my palm. Being a voyeur was one thing. Getting caught was quite another. "Well, I guess that makes us even."

"Hardly. I just saw your breasts. You saw a hell of a lot more."

Until this point we were both speaking to our computers, but now we turned and our gazes collided, his hot, slightly embarrassed but unwavering.

I felt like a pervert. "Look, I swear I didn't know that vent was there until I heard the sink and then..."

His full, sexy lips twitched. "You got curious."

"I went to investigate," I corrected.

"And stayed for the show."

We were openly sizing each other up now. I glanced at his lap. "Any chance of an encore?"

He chuckled, low and sensual, then his gaze went to my breasts. "I couldn't stop thinking about them," he admitted quietly.

"And I can't stop thinking about the show."

I heard his intake of breath. "Unbutton your shirt. Slowly."

I crossed my legs, clenching my inner muscles to squeeze the wetness there. Then as he requested, I began undoing the buttons, one at a time, enjoying the breathless anticipation. His own fingers worked on his shirt, revealing his smooth chest, the muscles proving he worked out regularly. When I reached the bottom, his face was slightly flushed and an erection was back in his pants.

"Now your bra."

One flick and the bra popped apart, revealing my cocoa-brown, grapefruit-sized breasts. My nipples were as tight and as when I'd stood in front of the fan.

"Now your panties."

I hesitated. He dared me with a raised eyebrow. I licked my lips and wiggled out of my size six, French lace undies. I stepped my left foot out and let it settle on my right shoe. With a light kick, I sent the purple garment flying in Jake's direction.

He caught it in mid-air, rubbed the crotch-wet garment between his fingers then pocketed it with a proprietary wink.

"Your turn," I said, my voice sounding breathy as I was already getting into the swing of things.

In a lithe move, he stood and came to lean over my chair, his lips pausing above mine. The contact of them sparked off a kiss that had me holding back a growl while reaching for him to quench my thirst. I freely touched his neck, his chest-- feeling muscle upon muscle, beneath muscle, between muscle. There was a slight spicy scent to his skin that reminded me of our lunch. I took my time tongue wrestling him, moving my hands down his body until I reached the weight of his protruding erection.

"Keisha," he groaned in my ear.

"Feels yummy."

"So do you?" He stood abruptly and tugged me from the chair. "Come on, I have to live out my fantasy."

"You mean, your masturbating fantasy?"

His teeth flashed in a grin and the slant of his eyes became more pronounced when he looked away. "Yeah."

It took only a few moments to set up the two fans next to an office chair that had no armrests nor wheels. Before sitting down, he slowly unbuckled his pants and let them drop, along with his underwear, revealing nice, muscular thighs.

Once he was seated, I leaned over and kissed his ear, licking the outer rim while he fumbled to put on a condom. The fans flanking us were blowing full on my face.

"Cocked and ready?" I teased, eyeing his penis, which looked like a beautiful condom-wrapped present.

"At your service," he replied, his hands already busy shoving my tight denim skirt to my hips.

I straddled him, more aware than ever of the sameness of our cocoa skin. The long, elegant fingers of his right hand moved between my legs, brushing my pubic hair and my aroused vagina with the elusive touch of a feather.

The movement soon became bolder, discovering, exploring the folds and wetness like a blind man with a new toy. His fingers plunged expertly on the way in and half-twisted as they came out. I swear to God I forgot how to breathe! I wanted to clutch him, with my mouth, with my sex. I wanted all of him in me right then.

"On your toes," he urged and I obeyed.

For some reason the pose made my passage a thousand times more sensitive to his manipulative fingers. I shivered, I squirmed, I rode his fingers in ways I'd never felt while masturbating before.

As if my whimpers were words, he understood my greed and withdrew his hand. I lowered myself on shaky legs, inch by inch, sheathing with his until the length of his penis disappeared into the saturated wetness of my dark vagina. I shifted my feet until my entire weight was sitting on his lap, my buttocks resting on his strong thighs.

"Ooooh, my goodness," I said shakily, the feeling of plump possession almost too delicious for words. The fan blades serrated my groan, making it into a hundred different replicas that sounded strange and infinitely erotic.

"Come here," he whispered hoarsely, placing his hands on my rib cage and tugging my torso toward his mouth.

I grasped the back of the chair and rocked gently on Jake's lap while he grunted and sucked on my left nipple. His penis was crammed hard, causing the slightest movement to ripple through my vagina.

"Jake," I moaned as I rocked again and again, feeling the sensitive lick and suck of his lips and teeth. He gave my breast a hard ,lingering kiss then moved to my other nipple. The breeze from the whirling fan cooled my moistened nipple, sending a cold shiver through me, which also made me involuntarily tighten around him.

He tensed, his groan becoming garbled. Against my breast, his teeth sank in a soft bite that was a pleasure-pain somehow linked directly to every erogenous nerve ending.

Cupping the back of my head, he kissed me hungrily, his hips flexing to speed the pace up a bit more.

I was cold and hot all over, the breeze created the strange thrill while the blades fragmented our cries, our breaths. Even the wet slickness of our union was altered by the fans.

"Jake. Oh, Jake!" I was close, so very close to cumming. Burying his face in my chest, he grabbed my hips and flexed upwards to my downward grinds. In less time than I would have ever imagined, I bucked uncontrollably, crudely, my shout becoming soundless as the orgasm ravaged me.

"Yes! Oh God, yes!" His voice sounded pained.

My crotch, still spasming lightly, was helplessly exposed to his thrusts as he also came, gripping me tightly and moaning between my breasts.

After several minutes of both of us breathing hard, his hands slipped to the curve of my butt and his tongue lazily flicked over my nipple, which was conveniently near his mouth. Every hot breath he exhaled washed over me long enough to be chased by the cooler wind of the fans.

His wristwatch beeped, and we both reluctantly glanced at it. The boss would probably come by in half an hour. I wearily rested my forehead against his spiky black hair and studied his face. His skin was covered with a sheen of sweat. Our eyes met just as his hand moved up my spine, causing a light shiver and chuckle. His smile wavered in a groan as I imagined his penis was feeling the clutching reflex of my laughter.

"Does Mac truly know how much of the project is done?" He asked, his left hand absently caressing my breast.

"Not really."

His smile was suggestive, his sexy lips curving into a full smile. "Good. There is so much more I'd rather do with you than having to meet deadlines."

I definitely agree!

The Storm

Right about the time I heard the overhead thunder, I was looking at the neon clock above the bar, wondering why I was wasting my time in the place. The evening had started out with the throb of the gathering clouds, looming with the threat of rain that came together like mourners at a wake. My mind and body were itching for more than dark clouds though. I was waiting for the spell of the storm.

The music was blaring, but the thunder was louder, and it easily penetrated the din of music, like the snarl of a beast kept chained and hungry for too long.

Having been stood up by my blind date, I could relate completely. First because I had spent most of the evening talking myself into putting on the tight jeans and stylish poet shirt, not to mention the trouble of having to carefully apply makeup since I rarely wore any. I felt like a fool for even going through this.

If Frankie Ali showed up this minute, I would drop-kick his butt and head out the door. Man! I know I was postponing, but still I kept sitting there, hoping like an idiot that maybe my date was late. I'd pretty much shot down the few guys who had come up, so it seemed by some male consensus that I was finally going to be left alone.

With a sigh, I sipped my Manhattan, but as I lowered my glass, I noticed a black man across the bar glancing at me. He'd been there about as long as I'd been sulking. As a matter of fact, he held the door open when I walked in, but he'd asked the bartender if a "Rita" had asked for him and I remember the bartender telling him no.

About half an hour afterward, I'd dared to ask the bartender about Frankie, but got a negative reply. The man at the end of the bar had given me a look that told me he sympathized, since we were both in the same situation. I didn't need his pity, so I gave him a cheap smile and looked away.

But now, with the thunder above and the power of it brewing in my veins, I downed the last of my drink and glanced at him, accidentally catching his eye again. This time he looked away.

Okay, he wasn't exactly handsome. And it's not just the booze talking. But if you took one look at all the men lining the bar, there was no doubt who the pretty boys were. The stranger's looks stuck out like a sore thumb.

About ten minutes earlier, when I'd gone to the rest room, this thin-ass sister had come in laughing with her friend, saying something about, "No way in hell! I know Sheila said Michael's personality is cool, but did you see how ugly he is? Please!"

It had taken me all of two seconds to know who she was talking about.

But now, looking at him, I had felt inexplicably guilty for not defending him. It was none of my business really, so I don't know where that emotion came from. Maybe it was the booze after all.

Now, I glanced at him again, trying to evaluate him. With the tight faded haircut, he actually looked like a marine who'd been in one too many brawls, but won more of them than he'd lost. His face had rugged character, his lips were nice and luscious, like LL Cool J, but the overall symmetry of his face was all blunt angles that spoke of a hard jaw, hard cheeks and hard life. Without a smile, his face was as harsh and as menacing as a bodyguard. His eyes, however, were as calm as a cat's. Sexy eyes.

If I was right and I would bet I was he had been drinking nothing but soda water all night. Kinda made a girl wonder what kind of a man would sit at a bar for hours and only drink water.

I checked my watch one final time and decided to head out. Screw it. I was too restless and pissed now. It's amazing how you can have a few drinks and still feel completely sober. I was feeling stone-cold sober tonight.

It was bound to rain, hard and heavy, but if I hurried I could run home before I got completely soaked.

I had actually made it to the front door before I found myself sighing, turning around and heading back to the guy at the end of the bar. Michael whatever-his-name.

Feeling this sober, I couldn't blame it on the drinks, but maybe it was the niggling emotion that kept pestering me. I just thought it would be cruel to let him sit there any longer knowing that his date had split.

He watched me approach as if he'd been expecting it.

"Michael?"

His eyes narrowed just a fraction. "Yes."

For a second I paused, caught up in the intense focus of his eyes on me.

"No, don't worry," I assured him. "I'm not your date. But I thought you should know she was in the ladies' room just a few minutes ago and I heard her and her girlfriend say they were going to go to Brennan's."

He just looked at me, making me wonder if he'd heard me at all.

"Well, bye," I said and turned to walk away.

"How'd you know I was Michael?"

Even though the thunder scratched the heavens and Aretha was bemoaning her blues on the speakers, I heard him. I should've pretended I hadn't. Instead I turned and tried to find a kind answer. Well, I couldn't say, "She thought you were ugly as sin, so guess what?" or "Trust me, she was pretty but sooo shallow." so I settled for, "Wild guess."

But those warm brown cat eyes of his seemed to have read all the other things. He nodded in a calm manner that indicated he'd figured as much all along.

I resisted the urge to tell him he was better off without the whiny woman, but in the end, I shrugged as if that was my explanation, turned and left.

Outside the wind was thick with the scent of rain, impishly tugging at my hair and shirt. It was several degrees cooler than when I'd entered the bar and the chilling nips sent shivers over me. I loved it.

Seeing no one around, I closed my eyes and inhaled the impending moisture, enjoying the moments of a storm closing in. I felt spiritual and primal, like I could open my arms and command the flow of wind, the veils of rain and the descending coldness with a wave of my hand.

The storm was alive, filling in my lungs, whistling past my ears. A rumble came at me, wincing through the air from a thunder that blasted from afar. The coldness sent a frigid lick on my breasts, and my nipples began tightening almost painfully, but deep inside I was starting to feel so very hot.

As every storm before it, I felt the instinctual need to revel in it, to tap the inexplicable magic that swelled uncontrollably in me.

My connection with nature was interrupted when the door of the bar was opened and closed behind me, the music barking before it was muffled again.

I turned to find Michael standing nearby, looking at me as if he didn't expect me to still be around. I felt suddenly self-conscious, my mind still semi-fogged with sexual stormy thoughts.

We smiled at each other like nervous strangers at a bus station.

"I was just leaving," I said.

"I figured." His eyes twinkled with humor even though his face remained stoic. Still I stayed and waited, feeling the storm coming closer, feeling him watching.

"Do you need a ride home?" he asked, and for some reason, he sounded like a worried parent more than a man making a pass at me. As irrational as it sounds, that grated.

"Nope. It's a short walk."

"I can drop you off."

Lightning whipped to the ground in the distance but the ricochet of thunder rolled toward us with a force that momentarily deafened the tundra. I let it roll over me, shivering until only the wind was moaning again.

"No thanks," I said. "I was taught never to take rides from strangers."

He smiled, his lips turning in the corners to show a dimple, which oddly enough made him look quite attractive, in a devilish sort of way. Almost reluctantly, he pulled out his wallet to reveal a badge. "I'm a cop."

I tried to hold back a smile. "So?"

He shrugged his massive shoulders, looking like I'd somehow managed to embarrass him. "Suit yourself but I feel obliged to point out the obvious. You could get struck by lightning."

The way I was feeling, I would welcome the rush of lightning through my senses. Already, the elements of the storm were evocative, and I couldn't ignore the scent of impending wetness, the harsh threat of angry skies, the alchemy of celestial magic. It never fails to bring out wildness in me, deep in my blood, making me hungry for carnal pleasures. I felt like a damned werewolf on the eve of a full moon.

Michael didn't move an inch but by the sudden shift in the depths of his eyes, I could see he was aware of the growing restlessness in me.

Then with a hush of greeting the first few raindrops fell, slowly at first, so that I turned my face to taste the droplets. Drop by drop, the skies released a light sprinkle that grew heavier.

I was surprised to feel Michael tugging me under the awning, but by then I was getting soaked.

"You're crazy," he mumbled, his voice rough and his eyes dark. I couldn't seem to quit looking at his lips. They looked kissable, lickable, suckable...

"Come on. I'll give you a ride," he said gruffly. Our eyes met and I knew he hadn't meant the words in the context I was imagining. But the image, once in my head, refused to disappear.

"Promise?" I found myself asking. Thunder growled from above, curling hotly into the pit of my gut.

"Come on," was all he said. Grabbing my hand, we half-walked, half-ran to his SUV at the corner of the parking lot. He unlocked the doors and we scrambled in. For a few more seconds, the sounds of rain pelting the windows mixed with his breathing and my sudden nervous chuckle.

95

But I couldn't keep my eyes off him, on the trail of rain that passed his temple, the firm lips, the hot gleam in his eyes. Definitely not an hideous-looking man. Riveting maybe, even tough, but not what any women's magazine would call handsome. Nonetheless, I found him sexy as hell.

The lash of lightning flashed closer, and I swear I was so revved with need, I felt like howling. I wanted to eat him up whole, to strip him down and take every bit of pleasure from his long, bulky body. I wanted to take and be taken by him. I wanted, wanted, wanted...

Doing the next best thing, I reached out, grabbed him by his jacket and kissed him on the lips.

He groaned, low and husky, but held back for maybe half a second, letting me initiate the kissing. Before I knew it, I was slipping across the distance while he pulled me into his lap where he tilted my head for a far more serious and thorough kiss.

Tongue, lips and mouths locked, nipped and tasted, dedicated to the sole task of discovery. And it wasn't enough. I wanted to feel him against me, naked, bare and hard with need.

Common sense battled sexual need.

The tiny voice of logic and reason was strangled when his hands cupped my breasts through the shirt. Expertly, he trailed his fingers over the puckered nipple, then rubbed the peak between his fingers as if the shirt didn't exist. Somewhere deep inside, I was on fire, melting, and the moans that left my lips were shameless with it.

"This is insane," I heard him murmur into my ear as we gasped for breath. "I don't even know your name."

This time the thunder made the vehicle shake.

"So?" I said, loving the mystery.

His eyes caught mine for a moment but then he lowered his head to my neck, finding the sensitive tendon at my collarbone. "So, what is it?"

Oh, that was so the spot! "I don't want you to know," I said breathlessly. "Not right now."

He ran his thumbs over the dampness of rain that covered the shirt over my nipples. I shivered. He teased again with that expert manipulation of his fingers. Heat from his thumb hovered right over my nipple, burning even through the damp shirt.

His hum was like a purr, nuzzling my jaw. Pleasure and anticipation had me turning my mouth toward his, but instead his head dipped lower, replacing his thumb with his hungry mouth.

"Ohhh, ohhh, Michael." My eyes slid shut, and when I forced them open, I could barely make out the silver blur of rain falling hard against his window.

"I only have one condom," he said huskily.

"I have one too," I confessed.

"Good."

And then we were kissing again, not sparing enough air to separate our mouths from the constant need to merge them. And it was this way, fondling, falling and tumbling, that we made it to the back of his car where the seats were missing but a few packing boxes were stacked.

Somehow, between the male taste of his neck and the hard muscles of his shoulders, we began undressing each other, using the darkness of the tinted windows to hide our urgent moves.

The occasional bursts of lightning worked like snapshots of hidden cameras, isolating a moment and imprinting the images perfectly into my memory bank. Freeze frames.

Like when his shirt was half off the roll of his hard shoulders, halfway down his flexed pecs, his tight abs in a half curl as he struggled to kiss me and shake the shirt off at the same time.

Or when he pulled my jeans down enough to see my low-riding thong, the expression of utter lust in his face. Or when my hand slipped into his underwear to cup his stiff erection and coddle it in my palm. Or when the bend of his body hovered over mine, his mouth absorbed in the task of sucking my breast.

Ahh, and then we were gloriously naked. The feel of his body was enhanced by the remaining coolness of damp rain and the heat of eager need.

"Hurry," I coaxed, wrapping my legs around one of his thighs and grinding my hips into it. At my hipbone, his erection was like a club.

"You want it bad, don't you?" he growled.

His voice was gruff, and I knew he wanted it as desperately as I did.

"Yessss." Running my hands down his spine, I grabbed his buttocks while rubbing my calves against his muscular thighs.

His hand moved between the press of our bodies to my sex. As he kissed me, his fingers pushed past my pubic hair, venturing between the folds of wetness and into my vagina. My wet muscles responded, eager to suck on his fingers the way my mouth sucked on his tongue.

Those thick, long fingers plunged in, pushing and rubbing in strokes that made me arch my spine and beg for mercy between moans.

Outside the storm was breaking violently.

"Please!" I gasped.

His touch didn't cease, but instead became more provocative when he matched his oral motions to his fingers. My tightened nipples were torment-ed by his chest hair, which curled soft and thick on his chest, yet brushed in a delicious abrasion. Every breath brought my belly in contact with his, and still he held my legs apart with his thighs, his fingers taking me into a spiral that was reeling like a hurricane behind my closed eyes.

"Michael! Oh! Oh, pleeeaassee!"

His reply was so low, I wasn't even sure I heard it. "Yes."

I lay trembling in the semi darkness while he hurriedly rolled on a condom.

"Now," he growled, moving over me. On a pulse of hard thunder, he pushed into me, rocking heavily between my thighs, holding me tight in the circle of his arms as his phallus lodged completely into me, long, jam-packed until our bodies were locked, woman to man, lightning to thunder.

We were the storm, harsh and liberated. Need drove me like never before, and I was begging this stranger for more, welcoming each and every ribbing thrust, bracing for the new, unknown pleasure that soared, gathering me toward a peak.

His grunts were like the gushing breaths of a racehorse, my own heartbeat like racing hooves. The sounds I heard myself making were too indiscrete to be moans, and yet with it I begged again, knowing no other language. The slickness of sexual penetration was a lusty sound, our bodies, sexes, sweat and hair all the contact I'd ever craved.

And then, with the potency of thunder, I slammed into my orgasm like a sprinter across the finish line. Mindless of everything but the vaginal spasms of pleasure, I lost my scream, clinging and bucking as the world lost its axis.

Somewhere in the beginning aftermath of my release, I felt Michael's forearms bunch against my shoulder blades as he cupped my head in his hands, grunted between clenched teeth and came in the lowest, most carnal male sound I'd ever heard.

A cadence of heartbeats passed before he leveled his head enough to peer at me with his dark chocolate eyes, then lowered his forehead onto my chin to rest. Finally, he moved his heavy body off me and lay sprawled beside me, on his back.

Moments threaded together in the song of wind-pelted raindrops. Eventually, I heard his gentle snores, making me wonder if now was the time to leave. But I felt too satiated and lethargic to move.

Thunder rumbled and as if he was having a bad dream, his hand suddenly twitched sharply, clamping on to my thigh. I jerked in surprise and he instantly awoke.

"Oh, sorry." He moved his hand away but I returned it.

He turned his head to glance at me, so I placed my hand on his thigh. Then I slowly trailed upward.

He smiled weakly, and I could tell he was a man who recovered quickly.

"Was that heaven moving or just us?" he asked, his voice low and quiet.

I wanted to kiss him for that.

"Didn't catch your name," he said after a pause. "Hi, I'm Michael, and you are?"

I let my hand caress his inner thigh, back and forth, not replying.

"Even if you keep that up, I'm too tired to"

My fingers curled around his semi-erect penis and tug-stroked it lightly, noticing he'd tossed off the used condom. "Really?"

The wind slapped rain against the car.

"Are you going to tell me your name?" he tried again.

I turned toward him and placed several light kisses on his chest. In my hand, his sex was hardening.

"Amazing. You're like a witch."

I sank my teeth into his chest for that comment.

He sucked in air, then released it.

I licked the mark my teeth made then with my other hand, I fondled and stroked him, working my way from his testicles to the tip of his cock.

"Still tired?" I asked, peering at him from between my lashes.

"Exhausted," he lied, "but you have a magical way about you."

I took that as an invitation to seduce him, so I did. Taking charge, I leaned over him and drank up more of his lusty kisses, until I had convinced myself that Michael's kissing skills hadn't just been a fluke. He was damned good at it. Damned good.

Then I took my time moving over his body, letting my breasts graze his skin, feeling the textures of his chest hair, the attention of his hard-on against my pubic nest and the moisture of our bodies. Sweat and sex.

I stroked, rubbed and teased him, at moments feeling as if I was punishing myself. And when I could no longer stand it, I reached for my small purse and pulled out the condom, making a show of putting it on him, measuring his long, lean penis with the width of my palm and the grip of my hand.

Joining our bodies for the second time was twice as sensitive. I lowered myself, inch by inch until our pubic hairs meshed and his hands gripped my buttocks to hold the position steady.

Then when I finally decided to move, I placed my hands on his torso and rocked against him, moving like a boat against the swells of ocean waves.

I could've stayed that way, feeling his eyes on me, hearing his breath stagger like mine, riding his lengthy erection for plunges that rubbed me somewhere deep inside, somewhere deeper that I hadn't been touched before. Every lift and lowering built the tension, sending it spinning at a new speed.

When I slowed down, his hands would urge me, when I went too fast, he would mutter something like curses and hold me in place. Somewhere along the line, I don't know how it happened, but I was no longer in charge.

I felt so vulnerable, sitting there, exposed, riding the wildest sex toward the inevitable finish. I felt so needy and naked, I couldn't even meet his eyes. Instead I focused on the quieter rivulets of rain as they drained down the wind-shield in tiny silver tears. But when he touched me, the image disappeared and the pleasure intensified.

"Mike." My voice sounded raw. "Mike!"

He kept rubbing my sensitive nub, causing my body to grip him with each thrust. The second orgasm wasn't as strong, but it was just as dangerous. It seemed to sweep us both into release at the same time, wringing out every last shudder until I collapsed weakly on his chest.

Pulling me so we lay spooned on our sides, we rested, or should I say, I napped. Rustling sounds made me open my eyes to see my purse nearby, my wallet in Michael's hand and my driver's license revealed.

"Jacqueline," he whispered as he read. The single word fell into place with the drizzle of soft rain. I couldn't help it, I looked over my shoulder and glared at him. Why did he have to know?

A dimple appeared in his cheek as he smiled and went back to looking at my driver's license, no doubt memorizing my address along with my other statis-tics. I wanted to hide, knowing that my driver's license shot was probably a sight better than I looked at the moment.

He closed the wallet before I could snatch it, and then placed a quiet kiss on my shoulder, saying, "I'd like to see you again. Not for sex, I mean."

I pretended to give it thought. "Then it's out of the question."

He chuckled. "May I revise my statement?"

"Too late."

He pinched my butt. "I'm serious."

"Look, Michael."

"What, Jacqueline?"

I loved how he said my name. Not calling me Jackie like everyone else did, but Jacqueline.

"What?" he prompted again.

How could I tell him that I was prone to storms with insane sexual cravings. That usually I was a boring person who was more often than not a workaholic. How could I explain that my occasional turns with blind dates always turned out badly? Or that I'd never in my life had sex as good as with him, but maybe that was because he was a stranger who didn't know me.

Would he understand that getting to know me would jeopardize the perfect memory I wanted to keep? This was me at my best, my wildest, my most brazen.

If we walked away now, I wouldn't have to reinvent myself, to pretend to be exciting. Something squeezed painfully in my chest. The everyday me was much more boring than this, every boyfriend I'd every had pointed that much out!

Unable to find the words, I simply said, "The storm's over."

His eyes sized me up as his gaze hardened. In a lithe move he rolled away and began to dress. Not sparing him a glance, I dressed as well, hating the damp tight jeans and the clinging bra.

He moved into the driver's seat and when I was ready, I moved into the passenger seat, my hand on the door ready to open it.

"Michael, it was --"

He silenced me with a swipe of his open hand signaling the end of conversation, the depths of his eyes still harbored fires of anger. "Put your seat belt on. I'm driving you home."

"No need. I can walk."

He gave me a look that told me he was really getting pissed.

"Fine."

Well, the storm had definitely blown over in more ways than one. The music of rain beneath the tires was a reminder of the deluge of earlier. Lightning had ceased and the thunder had moved on to distant places. All that remained were heavy gray clouds blanketing the sky.

He made it to my house in a few minutes, without asking for directions, which made me think he knew the area pretty well. Wearing a hardened expression, he walked me to the front door as if it was a duty, much like escorting a derelict to jail. Without a word, he turned and began to walk toward his car before he abruptly turned back.

We stared at each other as I tried to find something to say.

"You really had me fooled," he bit off. "I didn't think you'd be as vain as them."

"What?"

"I'm good enough for a wham-bam-thank-you-Mike in the dark, but not to be seen during daylight, is that it?"

I blinked, realizing he'd misunderstood my reasons for not wanting to see him again. "That's not it!"

He flinched, as if disgusted with himself for even bringing it up. "Forget it."

"I said that's not it!" I rushed over and had to grab his hand when he turned to walk away again.

He gave me his best cop face, revealing nothing. "Are you about to enlighten me?"

I nervously looked at the keys in my hand then back at him. "I'm boring." There. I said it.

He looked baffled. "What?"

"Boring. Most of the time I'm boring," I clarified. "Today was... not normal. I didn't want you to think I was a wild and crazy date all the time. You'd be disappointed, that's all. Most of the time I'm just sensible and boring." I shut my trap before I ended up embarrassing myself further with more insane ramblings.

He looked at me for an eternity. "Oh, that has to be the lamest excuse I've ever heard."

"It's true."

He gave a disbelieving snort. "Truth? Truth is that women like you need a good-looking man and not some mug-faced."

"You're not ugly!" The way he'd offered his remark made me mad enough to march to where he was and poke him in the chest. "That whole idea of beauty is stupid anyway. Look at me. I'm not hot."

"You're gorgeous."

I blinked, trying to determine if he was being sarcastic or not. Amazingly he wasn't! Wow, he thought I was gorgeous?

"Not even," I countered, then frowned at him when he looked like he was about to contradict me. "Anyway, not all people are stuck on looks."

He actually laughed and I really wanted to punch him for that. "Right now," he said, gesturing at me, "This is you being boring, right?"

I stared mutinously at him. His laughter subsided but his gaze didn't waver from mine.

Finally, I took a deep breath, damning myself for daring to extend what we had. I mean, he did seem like a good man, and sex with him had been mind-blowing. And maybe he wouldn't really think I was boring. After a start like ours, I didn't even want to think of yet another breakup where the reason was me being boring. But maybe he was different....

"Okay," I conceded. "But don't say I didn't warn you."

He stared at me intently then nodded slowly, a tiny smile curving his lovely lips.

"All right." I fidgeted with the house key, feeling suddenly nervous, then turned and walked back to the front door, unlocking it. When I looked over my shoulder at him, he was still there, the gray hues of a spent storm framing the background.

"Wanna come in for a bit?" I invited, my heart pounding double time.

That precious dimple appeared on his cheek. "Sure."

The Workout

The private gym was kept at a decently cold temperature, but since I'd been working out for almost an hour, I was desperately hoping someone would turn the AC down. Sweat was pouring down my forehead, down my back, between my breasts, but still I kept jogging on the treadmill, knowing I only had three more minutes to go.

My trainer/masseuse was Max, who was built like a bull. But he had the most amazing hands. The only way to describe him is to call him the black version of Mr. Clean, but I doubt anyone had the nerve to tell him that to his face. Certainly not me.

In any case, it was his hands rather than his physique that fascinated me. They were grabbing hands. Caressing hands. Let-me-have-my-way-with-you hands. Long, with wide palms and as obsessed as he was with working out, I wouldn't be surprised if he had sessions for those little muscles as well. Right now they were busy scribbling notes on a clipboard.

The only sound in the room was the pounding of my feet on the treadmill and the echoing breathing, declaring I was out of shape.

"Quit slacking," he said with a friendly smack to my butt. "Let's sprint this last minute."

Slacking? Sprint? I was gasping for breath like I was dying! A muscular stitch was definitely starting up on my side, but he reached to the controls and turned up the speed, like I was some sort of marathoner or something!

Truth be told, I hung in there, but that last frigging minute was worse than the consolidated twenty-nine minutes before it. When the machine stopped, I was sucking in air for all I was worth, not having enough breath to give him a piece of my mind.

"Are you trying to kill me?" I finally managed, talking to his running shoe, since I was doubled over.

Max chuckled and referred to the chart in his hand. "Come on, you know it will be worth it. Weights are next."

The man had no mercy.

I trailed after him, catching my reflection in the mirror and straightening when I realized I looked pretty wrung out. Someone once told me I look like Halle Berry, but at the time he was squinting at me over his kazillionth beer.

I mean, there's no resemblance, really. My hair's short, skin tone is about the same and I try to keep my body trim, but if you've not had your beers, you'd probably agree that I'm no Halle Berry. Maybe her third cousin or someone like that.

By now, Max had selected the torture device of the moment, innocently masquerading as a squatting machine, so I sat in the available seat and let him lean over me to adjust the settings and my posture. I liked it when he did this because I could smell his cologne and the lotion scent of whatever it was he rubbed on his shaved scalp and, of course, I got the perks of seeing his muscles up close.

"We'll start with sets of twenty," he announced.

He liked to stand in front of me when I did these, so I toweled my face, took a minute to ready myself and began the squats. The first few were okay, but as I progressed, I could feel the gradual burn in my legs and buttocks. At moments like these, I tried to imagine the fat melting, like grease in a frying pan. Of course, I had to block out the image of when I'm in the shower and realize that the fat has magically returned as dimples on my thighs. But for now, I was turning up the heat and thinking burn, baby, burn!

Max flashed a beefcake smile full of encouragement. From experience, I knew that the harder the workout got and the more I strained, the bigger the bulge of his erection would be in his tight biker shorts. There was no room to fake the trembling muscles of my legs now.

I'd given up the idea of melting fat, and although it's hard for me to think of sex during such muscular agony, seeing him get turned on goes a long way toward motivating me to squat a few more times.

When I was done with twenty, his eyes were warm with appreciation. "Twenty more?"

"Five?" I wanted to sound like I was bargaining, but Lord knows I was really begging. My ass was killing me.

"Ten. Start now."

I grumbled, hoping he hadn't really heard me. But I got as far as seven and could do no more. Not for him or the bulge in his pants. No more!

"We'll save those for later," he said, but I knew he didn't mean another day.

Undeterred by my wimpiness, he took me to the inner/outer thigh machine, his erection getting really sexy while I worked my legs. This machine was not exactly a painful unit, so I had no problem with it.

"Do them right or we start over," he threatened.

"I am!" I immediately complained. "Some of us mortals have weak muscles, Max."

"Don't give me that," he scoffed. "You've done these before." Then with a tender smile, he said, "I think you need the finger-grip test."

No complaint here. I rather enjoyed the finger-grip test and as I've mentioned, I'll do almost anything if I had sufficient motivation.

With a chuckle, he set aside his chart and stood beside me, running his hand over my small breasts, my bare midriff and into the tiny gym shorts. I knew my gym clothes look more like something a MTV video choreographer would wear, but this was the only time I could wear stuff like that and get away with it.

As my legs were in the contraptions that kept them apart, it was easy for him to slide those lovely long fingers of his deeper under the spandex, over the curls of my pubic hair and into my wet sex.

With his thumb rubbing against my sweet spot, he said, "Let's start with twenty."

"Is that the magic number of the day?" I asked a bit breathlessly. My nipples were already so tight, they hurt.

His thumb rubbed again and his two fingers twitched inside me. "Come on, let's see if you can squeeze my fingers."

I began the workout, pulling my legs together while working my inner muscles around his fingers, pushing my legs apart to work my outer thighs.

"That's right, baby. Clench those muscles. Keep sucking my fingers. There...again...hold it longer. Yes..."

I was hotter and wetter now, shifting my hips to get a deeper penetration from his touch, but he was teasing me and refused to give it up.

I forced my legs opened... Oh, Lord, he suddenly shoved a deep thrust that zapped through me like lightning.

I held my breath, enjoying the manual play.

"Close 'em."

I forced my legs into a closed position, trapping his fingers there, wanting to ride the orgasm that had started brewing nice and steady within me.

We kept this up in and out, open and closed. It's easy to forget your muscle aches when you get hand service like that. Goodness it was just wonderful!

"That's enough for now," he announced in a gruff, lust-roughened voice.

I actually whimpered when he removed his hand. But he made up for it by giving me a nice long kiss on the mouth tongue, lips and that wet sucking motion that had me sitting straight before breaking it off. I licked my lips and tried to pretend he passed muster, when I really wanted to grab him and take up where we left off.

Anyway, barely able to walk, I followed him to the next station, which was the butterfly press. Max adjusted the weight settings and I sat in the unit, wanting to ride the red piece of vinyl for all it was worth. Man, I was hot. Max placed my hands on the grips and I reluctantly started the workout, pulling until my elbows met in front of my face, then releasing until my arms were by my ears again. I did ten of them.

"I need to see your muscles," he explained, indicating I should take my tank top off.

Right! But I did what he says, because...that's Max, baby.

He watched me with a smile that was pure seduction. Then in his no-non-sense voice, started me on the second set. While I worked out, he circled the machine, finally sidling up behind me and cupping my breasts as I worked. Remember those hands with the magic touch? It's like some kind of sin...squeezing, massaging and twirling my nipples into ultra sensitive nubs of flesh.

My pectorals trembled and he noticed. "Last one," he coaxed.

I barely made it, but I had the sense not to let the weights clang on the release. Max hated that.

"Good girl," he complimented as he came around, kneeling in front of me to start licking, sucking and nibbling my bare breasts like they were covered with honey. My arms felt heavy, trapped in the armrests, helpless while he nudged his face closer, his mouth hungry.

I knew he could smell the heat of my sex, taste the saltiness of my perspira-tion, feel the slickness of it on my skin. His mouth lapped up my breasts, nib-bling and kissing the sensitive flesh until I was moaning in delight.

Finally, with his hot breath fanning my nipples, he said, "Let's get you to a mat."

Now, mat exercises meant the workout was coming to an end. I lay on my back on the blue mat while Max became all businesslike again, carefully stretching my thigh muscles by pushing my left leg until my ankle almost touched my ear.

Those fine hands gripped my overworked muscles, kneading and caressing them until he was suitably satisfied that I wouldn't cramp up. By now, the scent of my arousal and my sweat were making me even hornier. Max took a minute to grind the palm of his hand against the wet spandex between my legs, turning half a dozen slow rotations that took me damn near to heaven, and this time both of us were breathing pretty heavily.

I glanced down his impressive chest to where his cock looked like a massive root in his shorts, just wanting to get at me. I licked my lips and waited to see if he'd take the bait.

Putting his self-control into use, Max winked at me but turned me over and pretzeled me up to stretch my arm and chest muscles. At one point, his crotch was next to my cheek and I leaned into it.

Seconds later, he was stripping the tiny shorts off my body, pushing my breasts into the mat, spreading my thighs and cramming his fingers in my vagina in nice lean thrusts.

"Count down from twenty," he said gruffly.

I counted off, groaning, moaning but taking it because it was exactly what I wanted. Every thrust was a ravishing invasion and I arched my back for it, sobbing as the sexual peak began to form.

Twenty came too damned soon but unfortunately for me, I hadn't cum yet!

"Cold shower time," he said.

"No!" I didn't want a cold shower, I didn't want a count down, I wanted sex!

"Oh, yeah, you're right. You still owe me squats."

Lying down on the mat, he removed his shorts, releasing his man meat to stand out as thick and rough as I'd ever seen. In two seconds, he slipped on a condom.

Grabbing me as if I weighed nothing, he placed me over him, straddling his hips and oh-my-God-ever-so-beautiful erection.

Huskily, he said, "Ten's all you get. Starting now."

All my muscles that had bitched and ached suddenly felt in perfect working order. I gripped his penis, led him into me and slipped down his length like a mouth while doing my finger-grip test the whole time. He was so hard, he was jammed nice and tight in me, choking me with his thickness.

A hiss passed his lips, his hands gripping my hips and him pushing up with his muscular legs. "Oneee."

I rode number two nice and slow, gyrating my hips and working the long stalk the way I liked it.

Between three and seven I was coasting the edge of orgasm, feeling it close to erupting. My legs ached, my breath hitched, my muscles burned.

At nine I was desperate, wanting more, wanting this release that wouldn't come. Ten was a sloppy-wet thrust as he angled upward with a sudden burst of energy, ejaculating and straining so hard the muscles on his neck stood out.

The aftershocks that twitched through him did the trick for me, and out of the blue, I was catapulted into that magic moment where I couldn't think, I couldn't breathe. All I could do was sit wide on his cock and let the thrusts shake me too.

Finally, breathing hard and feeling limp as a noodle, I slumped over him and I must've dozed because suddenly I awoke, my body feeling cold.

The next thing I knew, Max was razzing me (although I bet he napped too), bulling me into going through the side door and into the secret massage room.

He covered his nudity with a towel while I leaned face down on the massaging bed, my teeth damn near chattering from the cold.

I heard the soft noises of cloth and water and it was like heaven to finally feel that hot, wet blanket Max draped over me, covering everything but my head.

The light scent of lavender filled the room. Raising a portion of the towel at a time, Max bathed me with a soft sponge and liquid soap. It felt so good, I simply enjoy the leisure of his services.

When that was completed, he began to massage me, using the lubricating oil, his agile fingers and the soft music of water bells.

All tension left my muscles, squeezed out by the warmth of towels, the soft spray from the water hose, the calm rhythm of repeated strokes, a serenity so deep that I mentally lapsed somewhere between sleep and wakefulness.

Turning me over, he repeated the process to my front, dipping into valleys, coasting over muscles that felt buttered. Mmm, those hands...

Then he spread my legs and I was feeling too good to complain. With the care of a physician, he gave me a light douche while I lay there still half asleep.

Once done, I could feel his breath on my skin as he moved closer to my sex...then the curious flick of his tongue, then...the oral kiss...

Being this weak and lazy, that kiss felt like champagne. I know it was not intended to arouse me into an orgasm. It was just licking and laving, teasing me into different realm of relaxation.

An obtrusive timer reminded me that our session was over and he pulled back, covering me up.

I heard him cleaning up as I stood on weak legs. Like a butler, he held up the robe for me and I shrugged it on.

"Max, as usual, that was excellent."

He half bowed. "I am here to please. Should I schedule you for next week?"

We shared a brief kiss on the lips, no tongue to cause complications, but enough touching of our lips to make the parting a new yearning. "Absolutely."

Car wash

I met Cameron at a bachelor party. Well, I had been the entertainment for the night, doing my routine as the stripper for a gang of thirty half-dressed men who, after a number of beers, behaved nothing like the accountants they were supposed to be.

My bodyguards looked nervous, but the men were mostly harmless, just gropping a bit. Cameron was the bachelor's best friend and so, his best man. He seemed the most sober of them all, maybe because he was in a wheelchair. I don't know.

My first impression of him was he'd taste good, like a hot toddy, to be enjoyed in several sips. That man sure was easy on the eyes, with skin like a mochachino coffee, light on the whipped cream. Arms like his belong in bodybuilding magazines. They were bulky and muscular, bigger than my bodyguards, which is saying a lot. His bare chest ripped with obvious strength. His legs, on the other hand, looked thinner beneath the jeans. Since the party was at his house, I couldn't help but notice the few trophies on his shelf of wheelchair races he'd won placed discretely on the lower shelves.

But I was there to dance and titillate, so that's what I did. With my demi-mask in place I began to move to the groove, taking off the sheer, devil-red nightgown, the arm-length lace gloves, and then blew bubbles at the men from a small vial I'd hidden in my bosom.

The groom-to-be took the vial and unsuccessfully tried to blow some bubbles back at me. With my eye-patch bikini covering scant territory, I began shaking my big butt, shimmying my even bigger breasts all the while the boom box blasted the latest jams. I think of this strip teasing as a workout, kinda like lewd choreography with few clothes on and a captive audience. Don't you know those men barked like dogs, hooting and hollering and coming up behind me, dancing like we were getting it on.

I made sure never to dance with anyone long enough to offend the bachelor. Those accountants danced like drunk puppets, but they sure took liberties with feeling on my butt. One freebie or two is fine, but no more than that. Besides, my gay bodyguards always give me a signal when it's time to move on to the next man.

I was dancing with the bachelor, starting on the final dance, when he grinned stupidly at me, burped and passed out on the couch.

"What the...?" I said in surprise.

"Looks like it's my turn," Cameron announced with a deliciously wicked grin. "That's what the best man's for, isn't it?"

Like excited monkeys, his friends caterwauled and hooted while the music changed to Marvin Gaye's "Let's Get It On." I glanced at my bodyguards, and they both shrugged, so I decided to give Cameron the honor of my final dance. But for some reason I suddenly felt a bit nervous, having never danced for a man in a wheelchair. But, hey, a dance is a dance, right?

Cameron seemed ready for me. His smile was wide and sexy, his voice full of low and sultry remarks like, "Yeah, baby... Come on... Shake that thing..."

He seemed to like the nipple patches, but since this party was now for him, I leaned over his chair and shook my boobs in his face, burying his nose in my cleavage while around me everyone whistled and cheered. I hadn't expected his strong hands to clamp on my hips and lift me clean onto his lap. I looked up in surprise to see my bodyguard give me a look that asked if he should intervene. I shook my head, letting him know I could handle it. But I wasn't really sure.

The second I landed in Cameron's lap, I knew the man had a functioning penis. It lodged like a hero sandwich between my legs, hard and impatient. I squirmed and did a grinding number on him, trying out my new-and-improved lap dance.

Up close I could see his eyes were more green than brown, his hair cut so close to his scalp I could see the glistening perspiration. And although I'd done many a lap dance in my brief career as a stripper, I was suddenly caught up in the moment, shamelessly gripping his tight shoulders, my feet barely touching the ground as I rocked myself against his erection.

I tried to block out the crowd, tried not to give in to the needy sensation of my crotch, which was getting wetter by the second.

"Enough," I whispered, trying to move off him.

"Not nearly," he replied then with his hands on my rib cage, he buried his face in my breast and licked a wet path between my cleavage with his tongue, plunging deep and following the ridge all the way through. The unexpected lick felt so incredibly good, I shuddered and rocked against him, moaning unexpectedly. Shocked that I had given in like that, I froze, trapped by the knowing look in his eyes.

I know I should've been grateful that the door slammed open and the bride-to-be stormed in cussing and yelling at the top of her lungs, but I swear, I sure wasn't.

Before I knew it, I saw a beer bottle flying through the air, a fist follow an angry profanity and all hell broke loose. In three seconds flat, my body guards had whisked me up and were dragging me though the door. As I glanced back one last time, I saw Cameron as if though a spotlight, unaffected by the spontaneous brawling. His eyes were fixed on me, one of his fingers touching the creamy smear I'd left glistening on his jeans.

Jon and Rocky practically threw me in the car and off we went.

"What the hell were you thinking?" Rocky yelled even though he was right next to me.

"Me? I didn't start the fight," I defended, pretending not to understand.

"Girl, you were this close to giving all of us a freak show! You've done this long enough to know better. You're a performer, not a hooker!"

"Look, so I got into it a bit," I admitted. "I just.."

"You got into it a lot, sister!" Rocky was craning his neck and rolling his eyes at the same time, mother-henning me by covering me up.

"Good thing we got paid upfront," Jon said, giving me a hard look from the rearview mirror.

"Okay, okay! Sorry," I said and turned to look out the window. I wanted to say I wouldn't do that ever again, but I kept thinking how good it had felt to grind against Cameron's lap, wanting more than just the teasing dance. I never sleep with my clients. Never! But this was different, right?

I mean, when he looked at me that way and plunged his sensuous tongue between my breasts, moving his head, his tongue trailing upwards...

Oh, man. Jon and Rocky were right. I was losing it.

* * *

Almost a month to the day of the fateful bachelor's party, I got a message on my answering machine for a strip dance. It was close to spring finals week in college, and my biology tests were not going to be a piece of cake, so I hesitated to make the appointment. But I recognized the man's voice, and more importantly, the address he left.

"Dress for a car wash," he said, sounding like he was ordering extra pepperoni on his pizza.

Determined to keep it professional, I called Rocky to arrange the meeting. Rocky called back and I could tell by the tone of his voice, he was already opposed to it.

"I called him," Rocky reported.

"And?"

"And he wants to get into your panties, girl."

"Quit mothering me, Rocko. Did he actually say that?"

"No. But I can tell."

I snorted to let him know he was being hennish again. "Can you and Jon make it or what?"

"Don't see why you need both of us," Rocky replied. "Mr. Wyatt says it'll be an audience of one."

That shut me up. Audience of one? Just me and him? Why even pretend to need a car-wash routine? Although that had possibilities....

"What? You've got nothing to say?" Rocky asked, letting his disapproval show.

"Rocky, I'm a big girl, you know? If I want to..."

"If you want to have sex with him, all I can say is that you're headed for trouble. In this biz, you should never have sex with your clients, but you already know that, right? I know you're a big girl and if that's what you want, then cool. But I ain't standing around to watch."

"Rocky"

"You only met him once. Don't know a thing about him. Sure he's got game, but you gotta decide what you want and whether you're going to charge him for it. Don't fool yourself."

I understood where Rocky was going with this. If I charged Cameron and had sex with him, well, that put me in a different category altogether.

"And you've got school to think about!" Rocky blurted when I remained silent.

"Yes, sir," I said meekly, smiling to myself despite the lecture.

Frustrated, he huffed. "You're hopeless. Just let me know what you decide," he said and hung up on me.

I thought about it all right. For twenty-four hours, that's about all I could think of. By the time I made up my mind, I was ready for the consequences. Okay, sex was pretty much all I wanted. The need for it itched clear to my bones and then some. I picked up the phone and called Cameron.

"Hi. You recently called Celestine's requesting an appointment for a, ah..." I rattled papers, trying to make it seem like I was busy looking for the message. "Here we go. A car wash?"

"Yes. A car wash." He sounded amused.

"I understand there is to be only a party of one?"

"Mmm-hmmm."

"How long is the entertainment expected to last?" Somehow saying those words out loud seemed to twist their meaning.

I'm sure his mind was in the trenches with mine as he asked, "Is this the only way I can get a date with you?"

"Why would you want a date?" I asked. A lot of guys like to ask me out just because I'm a stripper and they automatically think they'll get lucky.

"Why not?"

"I'm trying to run a business, Mr. Wyatt."

"Then charge me for the time."

I cringed, realizing I'd cornered myself into the tricky situation Rocky had hinted at.

"Is it because I'm in a wheelchair?" He asked with just a touch of cool disappointment in his voice.

"No. That has nothing to do with it."

"Then what?"

What indeed...

His voice became softer. "Your name is Celestine?"

"Yes."

"I like it. I... would like you to come over and I'll make dinner?"

I twirled the phone cord around my index finger, my mouth going dry. "Mr. Wyatt, why don't you just cut to the chase?"

He didn't laugh or sigh or try to play off my meaning. "I thought I was. Look, why don't you tell me why you called me back," he challenged.

"It fit my schedule and business"

"That's bullshit," he interrupted softly.

Silence was a tangible thing, crackling over the phone.

"Celestine, I want to get to know you," he said, his voice becoming a husky reminder of his tongue. "Okay, maybe I also want more."

"Define more."

"Is it necessary? Do you want me to be crude and say that I've wanted you since you creamed my lap and left me with a bunch of brawlers."

"Well," I said, trying to kick-start my brain. "That was certainly honest."

"It wasn't how I wanted to start this conversation," he admitted.

"I see." He was being fair and upfront, but I appreciated the truth. Especially after I'd been obsessing on him.

My heart beat like a tightly wound clock. "So, is this a date or... what?"

He paused before saying, "It's whatever you make it. I mean that. If all you want is dinner, then that's cool."

Clever of him to leave it in my court. "I'll be there."

He was smiling. I couldn't see it, but I could feel it as surely as the stupid smile that was on my own face.

"Do you like chicken parmigiana?" he asked suddenly.

"Yeah."

"Okay. I'll make some."

"Okay."

We sounded like teenagers awkwardly asking the other out to the senior ball when we were really planning sex. I found myself gazing at the ceiling, grinning while trying to think of something more to say.

He spoke first. "Nice weather."

"Supposed to be sunny all week."

"Mmm-hmm."

We both started chuckling at the same time, which seemed to break the ice. It still took us a few tries as we staggered through sentences, but before I knew it, we'd been talking for almost two hours. Finally, when I heard his call waiting, I decided to wind the conversation down. "See you Friday then?"

"Alright. Good night, Celestine."

"Good night."

I hung up, sighed and ended up sending Rocky and Jon an e-mail, letting them know where I'd be but pleading with them not to worry about me. Then

I turned the phone ringer off. Rocky, I was sure, would want to call and lecture me to no end. Jon would just figure out a guilt trip. I love them but I can do without all that.

* * *

I showed up at Cameron's house with a trench coat that hid my car-washing outfit tight white T-shirt and extra-super-tiny short shorts. I figured that the man had been looking forward to a tease and therefore deserved a show. And truth be told, once he'd put the notion in my head, I simply couldn't get rid of it.

He answered the door looking as good as I remembered. He had on sweats and a blue tank top that showed off his fine physique. His eyes were warm and welcoming, his smile a bit playful. With ease and skill, he maneuvered his manual wheelchair down a ramp to the kitchen where he was in the process of making a salad.

"Relax, take off your coat. There's a hanger in the hallway closet."

"I'm okay," I said, looking around. His home furnishings were modern and classy. I guess he'd hidden them for the bachelor party. "Nice place."

"I like to think so. Want a quick tour?"

I shrugged. "Sure."

The hallways and rooms were all spacious to accommodate his wheelchair. The living room was the ultimate bachelor setting, with a big-screen TV and a top-of-the-line stereo system. He had lovely pictures of his family, and several of his German shepherd, which he told me passed away a year ago.

He then took me down a hall where I peeked in the large bathroom and then moved on to a laundry room, opening it to look into the sizable three-car garage. All the way to one side was a van and in the center was an old 1950's truck that I rarely saw within city limits anymore.

"I like the truck," I said, admiring the coat of faded yellow and the faint dents.

Giving a crooked smile and what I could only imagine was a quick blush, he

120

said, "Yeah, that's the dirty vehicle."

"Ooooh! As in car wash?"

The gleam in his eyes got hotter, but he smiled and wheeled his chair around, ready to show me the rest of the house.

"Wait a minute," I said, deciding this was it. "What if I still want to wash it for you?"

He turned slowly, evaluating my coat with an assessing eye. "You're here as my guest, Celestine."

"I know. But I want to."

As eager as I was, I thought he'd feel the same and so I expected him to immediately say yes.

"What? Did you change your mind?" I asked when the pause became uncomfortable.

His smile slipped a bit. "Not really. It's just that... I've been thinking about kissing you all day."

I looked at his mouth, imagining the firm lips, the tongue... That long, luscious tongue... "Really?"

"Come here."

I knelt before him and he clasped my face in his hands, his mouth slanting over mine in a profoundly intimate kiss. His tongue was everywhere, lapping and laving mine, licking my inner cheeks, dueling with my own tongue until I was beyond breathless.

"Will that hold you for a while?" he asked huskily when we broke apart.

It took me a second just to process the words, but I managed to nod.

"Okay, why don't you, um, go in the garage while I, ah, lower the oven temperature. I'll be right back."

Still feeling dazed, I slipped into the garage. After taking a few deep breaths to recover, I found a bucket, which I filled with hand soap and water from a hose, making a nice froth that built quickly.

Cameron rolled in just as I turned the hose off. He carried towels and a boom box on his lap. When he braked, he put it on the floor and I noticed the start of an erection.

"So, you're going to dance for me?"

I reluctantly smiled. "Yeah. If you still want me to."

We gazed at each other for what felt like aeons. "I definitely want you to."

I hadn't realized I'd been holding my breath until he'd spoken. Feeling just a bit nervous, I looked around the relatively clean garage. "Mind if I make a mess here?"

"Not at all. I'm looking forward to you getting things wet," he said, eyeing me like candy.

I sure felt like candy. "You got a CD you want to play or something."

"I can get one if you want. Otherwise all I have is the radio."

"Radio is fine."

He pressed a button and J-Lo's voice filled the garage.

I walked up to him and lifted his hand to my coat belt and in my stripper voice, said, "Pull it."

He did. Slowly, with his eyes never leaving mine. When the knot came loose, he let the belt fall. I licked my lips, turned around and let the coat fall to the ground.

"Oh, nice. Very nice." The huskiness in his voice was familiar. It had haunted my dreams for many nights now.

Leaving the coat at his feet, I picked up a sponge, grabbed the bucket and began splashing the old truck. First of all, I had underestimated just how cold the water was. Damn cold! And secondly, I realized I was really going to enjoy this.

I splashed the water on the hood, then with the soapy sponge, I crawled on top and slapped bubbles on the windshield. By now my top was as transparent as wet paper and I had shivers everywhere, but I got into cleaning that glass like I was getting overtime for it. Having skin as dark as mine is perfect for wet shirts.

The hood was slippery, making me spread my legs wide for maximum traction.

Cameron occasionally wheeled around, taking in all angles and I felt like a model in a car magazine.

"That's right," he said. "There in the corner. Work that side... good girl... now over here... yeah, now grind your hips on the hood... woman, you're making me crazy... work it... work that ass."

J-Lo's voice was replaced by Britney Spears.

I sang, getting into it. Because my sponge had lost all its bubbles, I slid down again and refreshed from the bucket, then scrambled back on the hood of the truck.

"Clean the windshield with your breasts," he ordered, watching from the driver's door for the insider's view. I did as he said, spelling out his name in the squeaky-clean glass with my breasts while my shorts felt like they were shrinking and becoming a G-string.

"Oh, baby... hell yeah... you do that so very nicely."

He rolled back toward the front, his penis straining hard.

"Lemme see," I said, licking my lips and looking at his crotch still bundled behind the sweats.

Out came his cock, magnificent and hard, a prime piece of flesh rising from the nest of his pubic hair.

"Wax that hood with your ass," he said, stroking himself.

Legs open wide, hands gripping the edge of the hood, nipples tight and cold, I gave that hood a hell of a wax job, grinding and shaking and feeling the erotic pull of the shorts against my vagina with every move I made.

In his hand, his penis saluted, firming even more. I could see the tip of his penis gleaming with pre-cum.

"Get down here," he commanded, and I shimmied, going down on my knees before him. Yet instead of letting me suck on his erection, he pulled me forward, pushed my shirt up, reached for my breasts to nestle his cock between them.

He hissed hard and I realized he hadn't expected the cold.

"No, it's okay," he said after a groan. "Let me."

He began thrusting between my breasts, cupping them together to surround his penis. To assist, I bobbed up and down, too, feeling the thickness nested in my cleavage as he used the remaining suds as lubricant.

With a hand on my shoulder, he eventually stopped me, his teeth grinding from the effort. "Let me hose you off first," he said.

Weak-kneed, I stood and watched him grab the hose nearby.

"Take the shirt off."

I was pulling it over my head when the spray hit me and I screeched. He targeted my breasts, the water tickling my nipples.

"The shorts."

I remembered my stripper moves as I removed them. But even when he sprayed me front and back, it hardly cooled the fire in my crotch.

"Let me towel you off."

He toweled my breasts. I toweled his penis. He had me straddling his chair, his fingers invading me. I moaned and realized he already had a condom in place.

"Now?" I whimpered, my body craving sex like never before.

"Yes."

Those strong hands of his grabbed me and lowered me, my slick, wet passage stuffed with the force of his erection.

"Oh, fuck!" I groaned.

"Aaahhh, baby."

His mouth latched on to my left nipple and sucked hard, the sharp contrast of his hot mouth on my cold skin sent such a hard shiver through me, my vagina squeezed tightly around him, almost like an orgasm.

"Cam... Oh, Cam..."

I ground my hips against him, feeling the already tight penetration becoming even tighter. I felt such a greedy righteous pleasure. Every move caressed not only inside, but outside as well, where my clitoris rubbed his pubic hair.

By the time his mouth was on my other breast, his hands were on my buttocks, our bodies making slapping, wet sounds and the garage filling with our groans and moans.

I was so close to losing it, I wanted to scream. Suddenly, he pushed my breasts together, shoved his tongue deep into my cleavage just as I was jumping down on his cock. I came like a bomb, seeing the hot flash of orgasm exploding behind my eyes and feeling his penis pound perfectly against my trembling G-spot. I felt as if my vagina had become a greedy mouth sucking with incredible thirst.

Cameron's grunts mixed with the odd gagging sounds I heard myself making. Then about seven solid thrusts later, he bucked and almost jackknifed when his orgasm hit him.

I let the world reel for a while, relishing the feel of his arms around me and his hard breaths in my ear. After a while, I became aware of the cold again, of the sound of a small leak in the hose, of the thickness still plunged between my thighs.

"Sweetheart?" he asked, sounding as weary as me.

"Hmm?"

He turned his head and nipped at my neck, licking a trail of moisture still there. "That other car in the end is also very, very dirty."

Ghostly Touch

It's not that I never believed in ghosts, it's just that they've always been a sur-real concept I'd never had to seriously consider. And if I had any ideas about them, it was more to the line of plates flying out of the closet, spooky noises, revenge and that kind of thing.

It wasn't until I moved from Los Angeles and bought the old house in the rural part of Louisiana that I got to know a real ghost. The house was the clos-est I could get to the neighboring house, which was my maternal grandmoth-er's, a woman I had only met twice in my childhood, but whom I felt a strong link to. To my dismay, her house had burned to the ground in a lightning storm, but I loved the area, so when the Bakers passed away I held a small hope that their grandkids would sell.

It took a while, but they finally did. But by then, the place looked a mess. The home was an old beauty that much like my grandmother's house, had once probably been slave quarters. Neglect had left it looking crippled and uninhab-itable.

I had my work cut out for me with the thick growth of plants surrounding the house and clogging the road leading up to it. Vines crept all over it, out of control. Magnolias were like large nanny arms, grabbing the structure and holding it in a bosom so thick it was hard to see the road from almost any win-dow. And yet there it looked nested and comfortable in that wilderness.

Although I was renting a room in town, I traveled back and forth, working hard on that yard, clearing the vines until I could see a fine distance to the ruins of my grandmother's house. Even with the help of hired gardeners, it was back-breaking work trimming the intrusive tree limbs and creating a decent yard. There was a gnarled old rosebush that remained barren and barely alive. It looked so lonesome, I pampered it with a nice trim and good soil, hoping it would make it.

But despite killing a perfectly good lawn mower in the process, I'd made my mark in the yard.

I was much more careful with the interior of the house, hiring carpenters to reinforce the weak structure then really taking my time to restore the setting to what I felt would resurrect the soul of the old humble house.

No matter how many designs I looked at, I couldn't walk away from the wallpaper that looked almost identical to what had been pulled down. So I selected a pale matte of faded pink with cabbage roses faintly dispersed in the print. The furniture had to be antiques, bought in the region and, as one convincing dealer mentioned, was very likely to have originally belonged in the home. And with every piece I added, things felt accurate and right... familiar.

Then I moved in and that's when I knew.

There was a breath of a memory sweeping past me when I opened the door that Friday. I had barely passed the threshold when the feeling of being watched crept up my spine. Now it wasn't the creepy feeling you'd expect, or the jittery nerves you see in movies from psychopathic beings. This was the feeling you get when a hunk of a man gives you the once-over as you stroll by.

I remember smiling, feeling silly for blushing like an idiot when I was completely alone. Chiding myself, I shook the feeling off and hurried inside, intent on making the house my home. As I passed the furniture I let my hands linger on it, feeling the pull of something that drew my eyes to the muscular curve of walnut and maple. When the sunset put a hazy glaze in the room, the flowers in the wallpaper seemed to come to life. I questioned myself when I inhaled the scent of roses in the air. It was so fresh and real, I paused and frowned. Impossible.

I inhaled again, but this time, I smelled nothing but the oil I'd used to polish the furniture.

Telling myself it was my overactive imagination, I took my weary body to the old porcelain bathtub, filled it up with green mint bubbles and soaked my aches away.

Outside cicadas lent a lullaby, while lightning bugs painted the darkness. Inside, candles offered a soft glow. The water became a serene, tranquil sound as I washed myself, and when I finally settled back to rest, I felt truly relaxed and happy, not even caring when I inevitably realized I was falling asleep.

The dream uncloaked like a glimmering veil that I might have dreamed sometime before. Male hands, callused from hard work, were moving through water bathing me. I felt the song of greeting, of my body gravitating toward my male counterpart, eager with the first taste of carnal hunger. Water was more than fluid substance. It was as seductive as silk sheets, somehow brushing like warm rivulets of texture against my nipples, my skin, over and over, like a tongue, a lick, a caressing thumb.

The scarf of sensation moved over my legs, behind my knees, my inner thighs, rubbing between my legs, slicking up the honey of my vagina.

A single name found its way to my mouth, but I couldn't grasp it. I could barely wrap my tongue around it to say it, but it faded and reformed, the sensations of touch following the same rhythm of the elusive word...

The rude blast of the phone jarred me awake and I leaned forward abruptly, splashing water everywhere. Breathing heavily, it took me a few seconds to realize I had no lover with me. And that the angry ringing was from my phone.

Wrapping a towel around me, I ran to the phone, disgusted to hear that telemarketers had my number, even here in my little reclusive home where I had hoped privacy could be respected.

Even after I hung up, I glared at the receiver, battling the arousal still raging in me. With a flick of my finger, off went the ringer and then the alarm clock. No point in disturbing a dream like that ever again.

Dreams that erotic hadn't come my way in...forever. I toweled off briskly, trying to ignore the sensuous rub of the towel on my breasts and between my thighs. As I walked naked from the bathroom to the bedroom, I glimpsed at my reflection.

I was in the process of arranging my long hair into a bun on my head when I caught the peripheral image of my thin coal-dark body striding by. I was naked and yet I wasn't. The reflection showed a woman who had on a baby-blue headkerchief and a long gray house dress, small breasted and long legged just like me, taking the same stride I was.

The most jolting part of the image was the sight of the man standing behind me.

Bare chested and wearing homespun corn-brown pants, he stood with arms to his sides, looking like he'd been hauling bales all day. But his face, his eyes, were fixed on me, solely me, with a look so stark with painful longing and hope, I was struck motionless.

A rapid pulse lit through my veins as I stared dumbfounded. I could smell him too! Just like the roses, I could breathe the scent of him, faintly, like the freshly cut grass of my yard. The salt of hard-earned sweat still lingered and I could've sworn the sheen of it was still on his brow.

I blinked and the image incredibly disappeared, leaving only the reflection of my nudity and my face in a mask of disbelief. I whirled around, but saw nothing. Heard nothing. I whirled again. Nothing!

Amazingly, I wasn't scared, nor did I feel threatened. I just felt... watched. As a precaution, I threw on my robe, grabbed by trusty bat from beside my bed and checked every room in the house for a possible intruder.

Nothing.

"Am I going crazy?" I asked aloud, then laughed just because saying the words made me realize I was talking to myself.

Relaxing, I slipped on a light nightgown, closed all the doors and windows and flopped onto the huge bed.

I fluffed two pillows so that I would feel comfortable and half-heartedly tried to decide whether I should masturbate to abate the low-level hum of sexual tension that vibrated through my bones.

Easing my gown up, I placed my fingers on my clitoris, working the tension into pleasure that grew riper with every swirl of the sensitive bud. I switched between dipping my fingers into my honey pot and stroking myself and it wasn't long before the delicious orgasm blasted through my senses, making me feel replete, yet with the erotic itch that remained deep inside.

Despite my exhaustion, I still tossed and turned, feeling too hot to cover myself and not getting enough coolness from the fan standing at the corner of the room. I tried to clear my mind by watching the shadows moving stealthily over the transparent canopy above. And it wasn't until the thickest part of night that I was lulled into a light sleep that grew denser with every breath I drew.

The dream of rippling water came again, bringing the sensation of callused hands, silken scarves and a slow-kissing mouth.

That mouth was greedy, eager and clever. It began moving over me like rain, finding my weaknesses and teasing me just short of what I really craved.

I could feel muscle on me, too, bare and hard, male and lean, moving to align against my softer curves.

The first touches began on my ribs. The skim of muscle there sent a moan to my lips. A breath brushed my face, and I knew it was him. I could feel my hand twitching, wanting to hold him, but all I could gather was the bedsheet in my grasp.

His thigh settled over mine, bringing us hip to hip, belly to belly, human lock and key. I gasped, openmouthed, but his kiss was already nuzzling my ear, my throat, the deep masculine sound of sensual words flowed into my ear in Creole, Iriquoi or something dark and foreign, half-broken, but equally soft and intimate. A language I relished but could not understand.

A name tried to form on my lips but it became elusive, but I could sense the importance of it.

We shifted together in a sensuous foreplay, his hands moving to hold me closer, his palm on the small of my spine as his mouth finally, finally, meshed with mine for the kiss I'd been dying for.

That kiss...

Oh, it felt like I'd waited forever for it! It consumed me, filling my unquenchable need like cool, cool water. Our mouths mated insatiably, taking dominion of tongues, lips and trying to contain the sheer joy of reunion. It was the bold, heartfelt kiss of homecoming from a man who knew me very intimately and had missed me.

I yearned, I ached, I wanted him inside me, deep inside where I could feel the hard phallic thrust as it plundered my wetness again and again.

The foreplay seemed unending, carrying me to a brink that refused to rupture. I awoke to the awkward noise of my frustrated cry, my face pushed into my pillow in an unpleasant cotton kiss, the other pillow gripped tightly between my thighs, riding the crushed padding.

I realized the first rays of daylight were filling my room and... the bedroom window was wide open, the lace curtains blowing softly in the wind.

My blood was still running hot with erotic intent, but I was surprised enough to feel the countering effects of panic. I rushed to the window and closed it. Grabbing the reliable baseball bat, I went through each room again, breathing heavily, ready to swing if necessary.

But every step I took reminded me of the wet throbbing in my sex, the vividness of the dream. My heart thundered while I explored every inch of my home, but... on some instinctive level, I had an eerie suspicion that the stranger I'd seen in the mirror and practically made love to, was the one who'd left the window open.

This troublesome intuition went a bit farther than instinct. It felt too true to be questioned, and I realized for the first time, that I just might be haunted.

* * *

Hatch Gainer, the ninety-year-old man who lived a short distance from me, came over, leaned against my fence post and puffed on his pipe of sweet tobac-co. We talked for a good long while about nothing in particular and yet I enjoyed the conversation as if we were sharing a good meal together.

After complimenting me on the fine job I was doing restoring the house, he gave me a nod and, speaking in that leisurely drawl, he began telling me the legend of the neighboring houses.

"Your grandmama's grandmama, Sofie somethin-or-other, was said to be related to some king back in Africa," he said in his raspy voice, exhaling a fine plume of smoke that obscured his squinty eyes. "That woman knew things. Knew the secrets to magic powers, they say. The way folks tell it, she could make purple smoke from thin air. Nobody said much 'cause everyone used to go to her for medicine too. And that's how they met. Jake Muldoon had suf-fered a fever or somethin' and gone to her for some healin'."

Jake! That was the name that had tried to find voice in me. Why would it sound so familiar to me now?

Hatch was looking away and didn't notice my surprise as he said, "I guess word had spread about how she could heal this and cure that. But don't you know it, when she clapped eyes on that man, it was love at first sight."

He paused to blow more smoke out of his nostrils, and when he failed to con-tinue, I found myself asking. "And what happened?"

"Huh?"

"Jake Muldoon and Sofie?"

"Oh yeah. Well, now, they were in love, honey. They could hardly stand to be apart. Always seeing each other no matter what anyone told 'em. It was like he was Adam and she was Eve, and love was made only for them... It's just too bad about their parents."

His eyes twinkled while he puffed some more, obviously enjoying the sight of me almost squirming to hear the rest. I sighed, hoping to outwait him. He simply puffed and looked around at the landscape.

"What about the parents?" I finally asked, reluctantly amused by the way he insisted on stretching out the story.

132

His little body shook when he coughed, the exhale of smoke hitting my face with his startled laughter. "Why everyone knows about the parents. They hated each other. No one really knows how the bad blood got started between their daddies. But those men did everything to keep them two young hearts apart."

"Really?"

"Yup. Your great-grandpappy was a stubborn man. One day, he got his knife and threw it at the boy when he was running off, nicking him in the knee. That night, his daddy came back and busted up their windows. Back and forth it went for a while until one day, the boy's daddy set your folk's shed on fire...".

His eyes didn't twinkle too much anymore. "Guess he didn't know Sofie was in there, hiding. She died.... And Lord Almighty, Jake went stark-raving mad. Some say he howled so hard, his voice became the southerner wind that comes around here in the winter. Others say that a few days later, they saw purple smoke around the house for about a week and then... he disappeared..."

I suddenly realized I'd been leaning forward, wanting to hear more. "Was he ever found?"

Hatch adjusted the corn pipe to the other side of his mouth and gave me a cryptic look that said he'd tell no secrets. "Wouldn't be disappeared if he came back, now, would he?"

Having walked into that one, I chuckled, telling myself it was just folklore. "Of course not."

After a while, Hatch declared he wanted to get home before sundown, declined my offer to stay at my home and went down the path to his.

* * *

Night came heavily, perfect for sleeping like a baby. I really tried to sleep, but found myself pacing my home, rechecking the closed windows and doors. Deciding some wine would do the trick to break the insomnia, I poured myself a glass, put on some soothing music and sat on the couch to await my sleep.

Contemplating the hues of light in my wine, I wondered whether I was really being haunted. I mean, I'd felt whispers on my cheek at the oddest moments. And not only in the house. When I'd been chopping at the thickest grouping of vines the day before, I'd taken a break to lean against the sturdy trunk of a tree and I immediately had the sharpest send of deja vu, of having had my back against a tree while my lover nibbled on my earlobe. How could that be?

Three glasses of wine later, I was feeling hazy and more inclined to remain on the couch to sleep than to return to the bed.

I kept thinking of Jake Muldoon. What had really happened between him and Sofie? How come my mother and grandmother hadn't told me that story?

From where I was lounging, I had a partial view of the hallway, and I took a few minutes to admire the way I'd widened the room. The carpenters had done a good job of making it all seamless, going as far as to match the existing molding.

Then, just like before, between one blink and the next, I saw him walking down the hall toward me. His image was unfocused, almost transparent, but I could see him much clearer than yesterday. His gait was slightly staggered in a faint limp, his facial features fixed into a frown, as if it took effort to focus on me. With arms outstretched like a blind man taking his bearings, he moved down the hall, coming closer. I could feel his thoughts as if they were my own.

"Sofie!! You're here! Here! My Sofie..."

I gulped, forced to swallow the wine that had initially failed to go down my throat. The trace of his accent rang in my ears, immediately making me want to deny the connection to my dreams.

"Damned shadows are confusing me. I need her. Where is she? No, no, no. Not this room. There she is! Right there. Just to the left..."

I watched as he walked through the wall I'd had my carpenter move.

"What the hell?! This wasn't here!"

I closed my eyes, wondering if the alcohol was doing this to me. Would the wine create smells of wood and grass that were so real? I opened my eyes again.

He was still there. Coming closer, actually. In abstract amazement, I noticed how intent he was on me, so eager to reach me that he ignored the furniture and as a result, was walking through most of it.

Then finally standing before me, he held out his arms, the sheer power of deserted memories, wants and possibility pulsated in the short distance, waiting for me in that embrace.

"Sofie, come..."

"You're not real," I whispered.

"Touch me. Feel me. I'm real.... Oh, Sofie, I've missed you so much..."

"I'm not Sofie," I replied. No, not really. Not the Sofie he meant. I mean, I am Nina Sofia Buckman, but not even my mother called me Sofia or Sofie.

"Jake, I'm..." What? Talking to a ghost? Explaining why I'm not his lost love? And what was this pull in my chest, that glow that pulsated deeply in what felt like crazy recognition.

His face was so stark with emotion, I felt helpless but to respond. I tentatively reached out and touched the worry on his strong angled jaw.

A sudden release of power sizzled the distance between us, making me snatch my hand back and causing his image to become more dimensional.

We gazed at each other in surprise, then he reached out and set his hand over mine, palm over palm. Electricity arched from the contact, gathering strength as it trailed over our limbs. I couldn't even pull away this time.

There was a sudden wind in the room that swirled around us like the beginning of a hurricane, but I was lost in his eyes, in the way he lowered his head and kissed me on the mouth, in that long indulgent, greedy way of kissing that left me breathless. My world became a blinding rush of emotion and somehow nothing else mattered. From that moment, I knew that everything in my life was about to change.

We embraced as he leaned closer to cover me with his body, firm and strong, muscle and bone. The sound of static electricity burned off, crackling in the silence, and at the same time, I could feel the physical metamorphosis occurring.

He groaned in pleasure, as deep and achy as the creak of my bedroom hardwood floor in the morning. The physical contact was heavy and real, his ribs against mine, his heart knocking against my breasts, his legs certain as they moved to part mine.

I touched him eagerly, running my hands over the muscles of his shoulders, the short, tight hair on his head, the angles and planes of his faces. And still our mouths kissed until our hunger made us too restless to be completely gentle.

A nip on my neck turned into a love bite; a caress of his hands on my hips became a maneuver to remove my panties. We bumped against the back end of the couch, grappling with clothes to achieve complete nudity. And still he murmured my name, like litany between kisses.

"Jake," I murmured, feeling a newfound connection in a remote subconscious part of me.

"My Sofie..."

From the depths of a following kiss, I parted my thighs and he fit himself between them. I was so hot, tight and ready for him. Cupping my face in his hands, he pulled back, his nearly black eyes intent on mine as he shifted and pushed his erect penis steadily into my wetness.

"I've missed you... missed you..." he whispered, as if the power of his kisses hadn't convinced me of it.

"Oh! Ohhhh!" This was real! Real. Not some figment of my imagination. There was no denying his manhood lodging into me, filling me to the hilt.

His eyes slid closed as he rocked into me again, his head lowering for another kiss. I wrapped my legs around his hips, joining him in the rhythm of sex that so far had only teased me in my dreams.

Even as I licked his tongue, I could feel mysterious kisses dispersing all over my body, as if his mouth was in several places at the same time. My palms felt erotically licked, swirled signatures dampening the center of my hands, and so did the shell of my ears, the dip of my knees, the pad of my toes. And yet I was kissing him on the lips, arching my back in my desire to take yet another pelvic thrust.

It was amazing, insane and the most incredible sex ever. It was the kind of orgasm that defied time, hurling me to a peak that made me cum so hard, so wildly, so utterly uncontrollably, I was completely lost. I felt lifted by the wind around us, by the purple haze that threatened to make me limp. And in the end, I recovered, finding I was laying on his chest, realizing we'd somehow tumbled to the floor.

It seemed that as soon as he'd recovered, he was back to nibbling me again, kissing me, caressing me and murmuring those words I loved to hear but couldn't understand.

When we bumped into the coffee table for the third time, he moved to sit on the edge of it, hauling me on his lap where I rode him until I felt like I had lost my senses half a dozen times.

I couldn't get enough. And neither could he. When we weren't going at each other, mounted or suckling, touching or tasting, we were recovering and preparing for the next encounter. I felt insatiable, sore, and in that subconscious level, a sense of rightness came over me, refusing to be questioned.

Later, even though he nuzzled me, I yawned and slept peacefully.

"Ma fleur...."

The whisper lingered when I awoke to the smell of sex and the empty feeling in my arms where I expected my lover to be. I'd been covered with a blanket, and on the coffee table a single red rose, lush and in full bloom, lay like a gift.

"Jake!" I sat up and looked around, realizing the hard cut of sunlight was filling the room.

"Ma fleur," he repeated, "Tonight...." I followed the words from where they echoed nearby and found a very faded image of him, as if it took effort for him to maintain the visual form.

Then before my eyes, one blink to the next, he disappeared.

For a moment, I felt choked up with emotion, with a sudden anger, but then I remembered, he'd said tonight. Holding on to the word, I smiled. Air stirred beside me, causing the rose petals to flutter. Ah, he was still here, just not where I could see him. Was this how it was going to be? Could I only see him at night and yearn for him during the day?

I began to stand, then sighed and flopped back down.

Was there any possibility that what I'd drank was some moonshine wine and Jake was a figment of a wonderful erotic dream?

Experimentally, I touched my breasts, feeling my sensitive nipples. Then between my thighs where the intense sexual sessions had left me feeling tender and abraided.

As impossible as it seemed, I resigned myself to the idea that I'd just spent the night having sex with a ghost.

The far-off sound of a car caught my attention, the unexpected intrusion giving me the energy to move to the window to take a peek. The tan-colored Cadillac was coming up the lane, jostling slightly when it hit a small pothole as it neared.

Was that Parson Edwards and his wife? Sure enough it looked like them. Probably doing their civic duty of welcoming me, the newest spinster, to the church. Probably bringing a pie along with a spare Bible.

Hurrying I picked up my clothes and ran to the bedroom, grabbed the robe then ran right back when I realized the living room clearly smelled of sex. More than that, it had been my haven for it! How could I let anyone sit on that couch, or, heaven help me, even place anything, such as well-intended pie, on the coffee table?

A few rose petals fluttered at my feet.

"Jake," I admonished, picking them up then hurrying to open up the windows. I was grateful when a cool wind filled the room, dispelling the smell.

I seriously wanted to laugh, then toyed with the notion of pretending I wasn't home so that the Edwardses would have to leave. And then surely gossip would start.

Shaking my head, I grinned. What next? It was easy to imagine myself becoming the town's pariah, the crazy lady who lived alone in the old house and didn't like people stopping by to visit. Oh yeah. Children would probably take dares to peek through the windows and see me walking around naked, talking to myself, collecting rose petals.... Oh, if they only knew.

Tucking the rose into the pocket of my robe and quickly coiling my hair upon my head, I glanced at the entryway mirror to check my reflection. I looked rumpled, like I'd slept in late, which was perfectly true.

Arrgh! I also looked like I'd had marathon sex.

Jake's wavering image stood behind me and winked, the ghostly chuckle of laughter breathed close to my ear as a wind caress touched my butt.

"Jake, behave!" I cautioned again, fighting down momentary hysteria. I could do this. I could invite the kind parson into my house and serve tea and be civil. I could.

When the knock on the door came, I blew a kiss in the direction I'd last seen Jake, took a deep breath and opened the door.

Just Desserts

"Ingredients", JJ said, "are one of the most essential parts of an unforgettable dessert, don't you agree?"

I was laying stark naked on the huge, gray slab of granite that made up his kitchen island. The stone beneath me sent a cold shiver where it touched my skin, but around us, the soft, winking glow of candle light, set a warm, sensual mood.

"Yes," I replied. Above us, the usual clutter of hanging pots had been removed, but the glossy stainless steel holder was as good as a mirror. In it, I tracked JJ's movements as he stalked around the island in naked splendor. Every woman should know a man like JJ. A brother with night-water black skin, a cool, confident attitude and a creative mind.

He's also a talented chef at his restaurant, but occasionally, he calls on me, his 'muse', to help him come up with a new, delectable ideas for dessert. To me, he doesn't look the type who would be playing around in a kitchen. I mean, he looks like he's used to tackling quarterbacks or working with SEAL squadrons in covert missions. He's got that military look down cold.

Other than the 'Semper Fi' tattooed on his arm, he doesn't talk much about his past. I suspect it has something to do with why he's taken the time to smell fresh herbs and patiently tinker with exotic spices.

Today, though, I could tell from the limited items on the counter top that he was going to keep things simple. He started out with a wand of about five feathers, brushing them over my lips, my neck and traveling downward while leaving a very light dusty trail of what smelled like cinnamon and something else, maybe nutmeg. The sensation of the supple, tickling feathers are the softest of erotic caresses. Like a voodoo shaman, he brushes them over my breasts, circling one way, then the other. The process moves further south still, swirling over my navel in the same manner, before he parted my thighs and dances the feather tips over my feminine nub.

The rush of sensitivity was immediate and I found myself moaning and wanting to grind my hips into the whirling touches. But then, too soon, his movements roamed over my inner thighs in slow, provocative strokes, then wandered away. His eyes glinted with desire when he finally turned, heading back to the counter.

Next to the stove, he had already started the preparations and this time he approached me with a small jar of what looked like oil.

He dipped his finger into the clear, shiny liquid, then softly painted it over my lips. "Taste," he ordered.

The oil was ripe and almost hot, so I didn't need to lick the substance to know it was cherry-flavored. But I did lick my lips, because I loved the heat in his eyes as he watched me. The sweet-tart flavor was light on my tongue, reminding me of other lovely tart flavors.

"Do you like it?" he asked softly.

My pulse, which was already unsteady, picked up. Anticipation was building to an off-kilter heartbeat. "Yes."

With a slow smile, he moved the jar over my body, pouring directly on my belly button. The unexpected heat caused me to hiss and my muscles clenched beneath the oil.

JJ made a disapproving sound. "You'll mess up my art," he scolded.

"Sorry."

In our reflection, I watched the substance spill to my hazelnut brown waist before he moved the thin trail upward to circle each breast, creating a warm, liquid coil that led to my hardened nipples.

The jar was set on the opposite counter with a slight clink, then his hands moved over my body, palms splaying wide over my belly, making circular motions as he massaged the oil into my skin. The mix of hot and cold burned so sweetly!

In the reflection, his hands turned my skin into fine mahogany wood that gleamed as if he was an expert carpenter. The scent of cherry infused the air, but he kept working, massaging, moving from the bottom of my breasts down to the carefully trimmed line of my pubic hair.

It was the curious half-turns he did, turning his knuckles against the tremble of my womb, that made me feel as if I had melted honey forming inside me, a soundless sensation began humming in my veins. His mouth followed, but just to tease me, to brush over where his touch had heated my nudity.

With a low groan, he moved his hands to my breasts. I arched my back slightly to increase the contact, feeling his nipples in the center of his palms, closing my eyes when his long fingers expertly molded my sensitive flesh.

"Yes," I whispered.

Seconds slipped into each other while I reveled in the contact. It could've gone on forever...then his lips surrounded my right nipple as he tasted the first layer of his dessert. I moaned and cupped his head, allowing him to suckle until the sensation on my nipple felt too raw.

Not bothering to remind me about not moving, he lowered my hand, and shifted to the other side. I opened my eyes, and in the mirror I could see the dusky red of my nipple even as he bent his head suckled on the other one.

His fingers remained restless, moving in oil-slicked circles over me. I felt as if every bit of flesh that had been anointed was freshly sensitive, awakening. Especially my breasts.

Mentally, I begged for more. Audibly, I moaned.

His teeth nipped gently on the tip of my nipple before he said, "Okay. Next."

He turned away to the counter, his erection hard and proud. Several items were touched before he selected one. This time, he returned with a round, bottomless pie ring, placing it on my belly so that my belly button was at the center. His finger, covered in white, appeared on my lips again.

I suckled the finger, the way he'd feasted on my nipples. The sweet taste of powdery sugar dissolved immediately on my tongue. His eyes half closed, but he let me lick and suck his digit long after the flavor was gone.

"I like it," I said huskily, when he removed it.

He nodded, gave me a long meaningful look and went to work. JJ's face became a study of intensity as he took a sieve and shook the fine confectioner's sugar inside the wide circle. It fell as light as baby powder, and in the mirror above, it contrasted sharply against the oiled darkness of my skin. When he removed the metallic ring, a stark white circle painted my abdomen. A slightly smaller ring was placed within the whiteness, and I caught the glimmer of brown before his finger pressed on my lips again.

I accepted this offering, just like I had the last, tasting the unmistakable richness of unsweetened dark chocolate.

"Your favorite," he said with a knowing gleam.

I was breathless, so I only nodded and let his finger slip wetly from between my lips.

He bent and kissed my lips briefly. Much too briefly for me to enjoy thoroughly, but it was all part of his strategy.

The sieve once again hovered over the ring, raining over the inner circle in colors that ranged from burnished bronze to flecks of black. I knew the weight was nothing, but it felt like the pressure of something thicker and denser than simple dark chocolate.

When he was done, he removed the silver pie ring, then using a thin-tipped Kabob skewer, he leaned over me, drawing a primitive design in the sugar, carving gently into the layers that decorated me. The whirls and scrapes of the tip were intensely erotic sensations as the design of an ebony butterfly slowly was revealed.

When he was done, he looked at me, hungry like a wolf about to spring on its prey. He braced his hands beside my head, lowered his head and kissed me hard, his tongue plundering, letting me know just how ravenous he was.

We broke off panting, but his lips worked their way to my ear, by my short hair, and I shuddered with need, watching in the metal above as his muscles rippled when he moved.

His tongue circled the shell of my ear, licked the softness of my earlobe, bit it gently, then exhaled raggedly as if he thought he was losing control.

Abruptly, he stepped back and walked back to his ingredients. A whoosh of a flame came from the stove, I turned my head and watched my naked chef open the oven and pull out a small double boiler, placing it over the flames. Immediately, the rich scent of chocolate mingled and intertwined with the delicate cherry from earlier and the light essence of cinnamon.

JJ stirred a wooden spoon in the double boiler, looking like a nude witch doctor with his brew. He raised the spoon and the dark satin finish of chocolate slipped back into the pot. He dripped a bit on his open palm, blew on it then licked his hand clean. I'm sure he knew I was watching, but I still felt like a voyeur. My gaze dropped to his penis when it sustained a firm upward angle, looking hard and stiff as a weapon.

Good. I was glad to know I wasn't the one suffering.

JJ turned the flame off, moved the pot to a cooler section and poured a big dollop onto a shallow saucer. I turned my attention back to the stainless steel above me, but I could hear utensils clicking quietly together as he selected one of them.

His large feet came into my reflected view, then his charging penis, followed by his lean body and slightly crooked grin.

When he reached the island, he tested the heat of the chocolate again, the with a wink and a wide grin, he lifted his dipped finger to my lips. The heat stung my lips, but the chocolate was absolutely heavenly. This singular flavor easily blended the cherry oil and sugars from earlier, forming a distinct taste that was like an aphrodisiac. I rolled the flavor around in my mouth, realizing he'd mixed in just a pinch of hot pepper that left a piquant, lover-like aftertaste.

I licked my lips twice, and by the look in his eyes, I knew no words of approval were needed from me.

He spooned a satin ribbon of hot chocolate from the edge of my painted navel on upward in a semi-scorching path that was a kiss of another kind. It tensed in my spine and sustained a bite on my skin. The drizzled of hot liquid made its way to my left breast where it circled slowly into the nipple. The chocolate was definitely hot, just short of burning my sensitive flesh. I clenched my teeth together to hold back a cry.

The wetness from my womb leaked between my thighs, and even the cool stone beneath me wasn't helping.

I kept my eyes tightly closed, nibbling on my lower lip and concentrating on my breathing while he continued the process on my right breast.

"You okay?" he whispered.

"Yeah," I managed.

Just when I thought he was done, he started again, retracing the existing trail with more chocolate. Every breath was like a culinary bouquet, every trail of chocolate satin was a lovers branding.

I concentrated on the heat when it shifted back to my belly, sensing he was creating some sort of design along the border of the butterfly.

"Beautiful," he whispered.

I opened my eyes and watched him watching me. He seemed pretty proud of his artwork on the canvas of my body and personally, despite the tattoo of a heat still on my skin, I thought it was one of his best works too.

The antennae of the intricate butterfly had become the decorative trail of chocolate on my breasts. JJ turned back with a mug filled with whipped cream. I was enjoying that smell when he carefully placed two small, very cool, peaks on my nipples. The contrast of brisk coolness against what had been sustained heat, made me shiver and skirt the edge of an orgasm.

I moaned wondering if he was going to add more, but he didn't.

I could hear his unsteady breathing as he returned to his ingredients. He came back with a smile and fingers coated in granules of sugar. With infinite care, he sprinkled them over my body, then bent and in about a dozen licks, he removed the white crests of the melting cream from my breasts.

Since I knew the granulated sugar had been the final touch, I moved my hand until it touched his lean thigh. He half-turned and his erection jutted right into my hand. So, I obliged him by stroking his thickness from testicles, up the length of his arousal, to the taut tip.

Our shallow breathing was like some sort of chant in the echoing room. And because I was so close, the fleshy friction sound of my palm on his penis was an even more sensuous sound.

Wordlessly, I pumped and milked him, my thumb rubbing a vein that stood out more and more, until a white-glaze pre-cum appeared at the tip of his cock. When his hand clamped over mine and stilled it, I reluctantly released him.

In a panther-like move, his thigh muscles flexed and he jumped onto the island, straddling me, his penis jutting outward, primal.

"Think it will work?" I asked.

"If you follow the rules, it will," he said then he nudged my thighs apart and held himself, push-up style, over me. Military muscles showed no weakness as the seconds passed. They looked even more impressive from the reflection above.

"Let's do it," I whispered.

JJ lowered himself, inch by inch, his velvety brown eyes hypnotic as they held my gaze. I didn't need to look up to know his butt muscles were flexing, his cock docking into the wet portal of my sex like a loaded missile. I was pushed against the granite when his weight came on me, sealing the artwork and our sexes in one smooth move.

I gasped, riveted in the pleasure of what I'd been anticipating all evening.

That intimate, physical linking, that control of passion was a powerful, unleashing rush like no other.

He more than physically filled me.

I could smell the ingredients blend with body heat, with the scent of needs, of man and woman. I could feel the throb of his erection so deep inside, my womb gripped it greedily.

With my breath stuck in my throat, I felt his arms slip under my shoulders and cup my head, his hips flexing into a delicious stroke that sent a surge of quivering pleasure me over.

JJ inhaled my weak moan and sealed my mouth with a kiss.

I knew we were supposed to make love as slowly as possible, to transfer the image from my body to his, but the urge to pound out a rhythm was almost overwhelming. Besides, control was the whole point.

In the mirror above, it looked like idle sex, but it required concentration, movement of internal muscles and mental restraint. It was all about prolonging the pleasure. And it was utterly, completely mind-bending.

I clung to his shoulders and moved slightly beneath him, feeling crystals of sugar digging into my skin. The slickness of chocolate was still hot, and the light cherry oil made the butterfly in my navel tremble against the trap of desire.

He moved again. Half in. Half out.

My thighs rubbed his restlessly when he kissed me again, deeper, his tongue matching the penetration of our bodies. We rocked like idle ocean waves on tropical shores, like summer wind over calm wheat fields, like the tempo of a slow dance.

Refining the move, JJ sustained a longer thrust at every other push, grinding his pelvis into mine.

"Oh!" I exclaimed, feeling my sex stroked harder by each movement.

I tensed even more and my internal muscles, slippery and tight, shivered around him. The countdown had begun. I knew I wouldn't last another minute, so I clasped his hips with my knees and rode his stiff, unmoving body until the waves crashed me into a dissolving mindscape.

I was panting hard when his arms tightened around me and his body abruptly pinned me hard against the stone. His teeth sank gently into my neck, his orgasm an almost silent growl. His body, however, jerked and pumped with barely leashed control.

I lay there, spent, covered in a sheen of sweat and feeling like a jelly-filled pastry. I ran my hands over the damp, contoured ridges of his back, and after a while, he raised his head, grinning at me.

"How do you think we did?" he asked.

I smiled, but made a doubtful expression. He chuckled.

"Let's see."

The stone now felt warm. We shifted, trying to keep our torso's together while changing positions. I giggled and clutched his buttocks to keep from separating and slipping to the ground like a pancake. Finally, we managed it, and I carefully lifted myself from him, leaning back until my thighs straddled his and only our joined sexes still connected us.

"Success!" I said, looking down at him. Sure, the intricate design was gone, but a decent copy of the circles, butterfly and chocolate were preserved against his body.

JJ was checking it out on the stainless steel, intently looking at the messy transfer like a psychic studying some tea leaves. His fingers hovered over the outline of the transfer, until he was satisfied. "Yeah. You did good this time."

"Why, thank you. Practice makes perfect."

"Who cares about perfection when the practice is where the fun is?" he teased.

I chuckled then bent over and licked a trail of peppery hot chocolate from his ribs. Yum! The granules of white sugar had become tiny translucent crystals, which started me hunting all over his chest for them. I worked my tongue until it ached, running it across his warm, hard muscles, delighting in the taste of his skin, chocolate (in its various flavors(and sucking his skin every now and then for that extra taste of cherry. I made my way down his contours to his belly where I could hardly curl over enough to finish my dessert.

Between my thighs, his penis twitched, telling me it was recovering nicely.

"My turn," JJ said, leaning up on his elbows to bring his mouth to my breasts.

Now, JJ has always eaten as if I really am a served up meal, which I guess I am. His lips and tongue were devious and meticulous, stroking, tasting and re-tasting some spots over and over.

My nipples, the most sensitive links to what makes me weak, belonged to the stroke of his mouth, to the touch of his hands. His palms cruised back down, invading the folds of my wet sex around the flank of my buttocks, then back around, moving upward, brushing against crumbs of powdered sugar which he licked into his mouth almost absently while crossing over between breasts.

Five minutes turn into ten before his mouth found mine again. His face was sweet and sticky, and his erection was a strong shaft inside me.

I made him lean back again on his elbows, then started to ride him. From experience, I knew this could get slightly painful on the knees, so I touched my still sensitive clit to speed up the process.

"Yes, baby," he encouraged huskily.

This time, there was new freedom to move where I hadn't before, so I moved on him with less restraint, taking as much as I wanted. My thighs shook from the strain, my cries became jagged, and my knees were in agony, but I refused to stop.

When I did cum, I felt the world of candlelight shift dizzily around me, and in that lightheaded moment, I felt him striving for his own release for almost another minute before he grunted my name and came too.

I collapsed on his chest, my head bobbing with the billowing movements of his chest, hearing his racing pulse on the sticky skin against my ear. Boy, did we ever need a shower.

After a while, JJ said, "Dinner tomorrow?"

"Sure."

Since, I was a regular patron at the restaurant, I knew our little secret would be shared in a speaking glance tomorrow, when he would pretend to be a chef who was simply giving his preferential attention to me, a food critic for the local newspaper.

I would, of course, accept the honorary first piece of dessert and by scent alone, I'd start remembering every detail of its creation. As often as he's used chocolate in recipes, the collective power of those memories are enough to make me moan at the first bite of the dessert.

Afterward, those within earshot would hear my polite praise when I declare him a genius for coming up with such an extraordinary and delectable dessert...